Up for

Crystal Santoría

authorHOUSE®

AuthorHouse™
1663 Liberty Drive
Bloomington, IN 47403
www.authorhouse.com
Phone: 1 (800) 839-8640

Published by AuthorHouse 04/12/2016

ISBN: 978-1-5246-0209-3 (sc)
ISBN: 978-1-5246-0207-9 (hc)
ISBN: 978-1-5246-0208-6 (e)

Library of Congress Control Number: 2016905569

Print information available on the last page.

In memory of Stephon "Papa" Mitchell, thank you for stepping up to be the father God knew I needed. I love you always and forever.

Contents

Ch. 1

D.J. Drill: That was Every Moment by Jodeci. You're on the air with D.J. Drill and our special guest Cristina aka Cris.

Cristina: Good morning, good to be here.

D.J. Drill: I see you're on tour with your spoken word doing your thang out here in the Atl. Word going around is that you are turning some of your work into music aye? Crossing over I hope?

Cristina: Yes, the tour is going great. I'm actually performing tonight at the opening of my club C.S. Café I'm Burmingham. I am working on a few things with the music. I don't want to spill everything. I'll just keep y'all guessing.

D.J. Drill: Ouch, don't leave me hanging. (She started laughing)

Cristina: Have to leave something until it's finished, right?

D.J. Drill: Right… Right… Well, we have a lot more to talk about but we'll be right back. Keep it locked on WBHX 105.8 Jams.

> We went off the air and chatted for a little while. D.J. Drill was a model built woman. She got the name from her times in the army. They say she was the toughest female soldier.

1

She left the military after her parents died in a plane crash. We just shared some laughs and vodka before we went back on the air.

D.J. Drill: We're back on WBHX 105.8 Jams. If you're just tuning in, we're sitting with the lovely Cris. How has this journey of spoken word tours, acting, and opening a poetry café going?

Christina: It's been a long hard journey. I'm glad to be here. I never thought I would be this far in. These few years have been hell in a nutshell. Between personal drama to losing one of my best friends, I almost broke to the point where I didn't want to do this. I wanted to just give up completely.

D.J. Drill: You didn't and that's a good thing.

Cristina: No I didn't! I had to suck it up and be strong. I had to make it the "right way" by any means necessary. I owed that to myself.

D.J. Drill: I'm glad you never gave up. It was glad having you here today so where do people need to go tonight?

Cristina: C.S. Café in Birmingham, Alabama is where it's at. An explosive amount of talent and I of course will be there. Doors open at 7 so get there early.

D.J. Drill: We'll be giving away tickets to the tenth caller. It was nice having you here Cris.

Cristina: Good to be here.

D.J. Drill: Well taking us out is a little Jamie Foxx "You Changed Me". Keep it locked, this is 105.8 WBHX Jams. Head out to C.S. Café tonight. We're out!

We were off the air finally. I had about three more stops before I had to get ready for tonight. All I needed was some liquor. I just needed something strong to ease my mind. It was driving me crazy how much I had lost within a year. I cried every time I thought of Sara. It wasn't supposed to be this way. I stopped to take a deep breath before I just couldn't stop myself from crying all over again. I told myself these were happy tears but I knew better. I'm happy to be in this position but I just couldn't shake my mind off of anything. I had gotten myself together and started driving until I pulled up in my driveway. My house was just a two story dollhouse type, three car garage, pool/Jacuzzi, five bedrooms, three and a half bath, and a big kitchen. The kitchen is what I really looked for when I bought it. I loved to cook. I just kicked off my heels as I entered the house. The phone started ringing but I already knew it was mom so I'll just call her back later. My mom and I have a very close relationship. I didn't even get to my bedroom before I started stripping down in the living room. No one was here but me anyway. I ran upstairs and started to turn the shower on. I had my hair in eight big twists. I had returned natural like almost four years ago. The water from my bedroom bathroom was steaming hot. It was just what I needed to relax before tonight. I needed something else but that was a whole different topic. I stepped in the shower with my back to the shower head and let the water drip down my neck and all through the slit of my ass. Pulling out my dove body wash and loufa and started the cleanliness ritual. I wished I could have stayed in there for much longer. My phone rang and that ringtone was not mom's so it must be someone else. I stepped out of the shower after turning it off. I had rubbed down in baby oil gel before I got out so my body had little raindrops of water and oil smoothly running down it. My boobs were double d and I had a big booty. I didn't care as long as genetics had blessed me. I am thankful for that. I checked my phone and to my surprise it was the one I never wanted to hear from. Years of back and forth, I just didn't want to welcome that back in my space so I sent it to voicemail. Checking my closet for what I was going to wear tonight,

I could hear Sara say, "Gold baby, because gold and white are for goddesses". I decided to wear my gold dress with the white heels. This was going to be the second time that I stepped on the stage after all that went down. I dried off and put my outfit on. I took down my twists and put on some gold eyeshadow and red lipstick. After I had finished prepping, I locked up and got back in my car. As I was pulling up, standing outside was Jennifer. I took a deep breath and tried to mask what I was thinking.

"Hey girl, I haven't seen you in like forever." She said.

"You know how things go, just been busy".

I really didn't want to have a conversation with her right now. This was not the time or the place. I continued to walk inside the venue and to my dressing room. As I got my thoughts together, in walks my agent and manager, Daniel and David.

"Are you ready to get it popping in here?" David said.

I really am nervous because after all that went down, I just want a good night. I need this to go over without a hitch.

Daniel said, "Everything will be as it is." Carpe Diem!

I took a deep breath and we all bowed our heads and prayed. I seem to feel at ease when I pray. My mom walks in the room and peace just fell.

"I'm glad you made it here"

"I wouldn't miss it for the world", she said.

"You better take your seats before it gets too crowded.

"I'm not worried about that. Even if I have to stand off stage I will see my baby perform", She said.

"I'm not a baby anymore mom."

"I don't care how old you get, even if you are fifty, you will still be my baby." she said.

Everyone took their seats and I waited till the host greeted everyone and introduced me. I felt so hot like I had never been on stage before. As long as I can remember, I've never shyed away from being on stage. Theatre and singing has always been something I naturally did. When he introduced me, my heart started racing and I slowly walked on stage.

4

"What's up Birmingham?! Thank you all for coming out here tonight. I'm so excited to be standing here at the opening of my own poetry café. Well I won't let you wait for much longer. This piece is called "*Sold*"."

I thought about everything that had transpired in the past and closed my eyes and started to speak.

"There are others sold. Many slave systems to get banked off on. Lineages sold... Snatched up on sidewalks... Sold on black markets... Worthless, worth less than a five dollar footlong, that dollar menu from McDonalds, but forced to lie with thieving strays who stay up all night just to taste the crevices of our down unders. Making us mothers way before our time... Pussies only sold to control the mind. Give you a little taste then every time you crawl back they skyrocket the rate. Sold! Worthless, worth less than that ammonia based golden shower he rained down on my face. Sold! Like a caged bird, I'm sold. At times I have the opportunity to be free but my papers of slavery are his fists pounding against me and memories slip too quickly so I stay caged. Sold! Who could really save me anyway? How much? How much for her release? You can buy ten times the sheep but that won't make them leave. Take me! Take me! I'll replace her! They said, "You're too close to the grave to let this one be replaced." Sold! Stuck too far in my own fears to ever let myself go... Sold! Traded to the next highest bidder based off assets genetics made waiting days to escape. Sold! Another part of history left untold because I might not live to build nations foretold. No screaming too bold because once enslaved in my mind, freedom is not there to reach. Justice won't be there to set me free. Sold! Enslaved to the mind!—"

Ch. 2

Everything wasn't a fairytale. A year and a half ago, my world was starting to get better and worse at the same time. Speak of the devil as to how it all began. Tyler is calling my phone. I answer.

"Hello", I said.

"Hey, what are you doing tonight?" he said.

I already knew where this was headed but I entertained it anyway.

"Nothing much, just a glass of wine and music, I replied.

Tyler was a six foot two chocolate man with a king monty. His smile was so contagious that he could tear down brick walls just by smiling.

"I'll wait up for you if that's what you're insinuating? I said.

"You don't have to wait that long seeing that I'm outside your door. Just let me in" he said.

Tyler had this thing about showering that I couldn't explain. I had just turned the water on before I went downstairs to open the door. I stood there in a towel I was going to wash anyway.

"Good evening" I said.

He didn't reply. He just walked in the house and unraveled the towel as it dropped to the floor. I knew where this was headed and although my spirit was saying no, I did it anyway. He started kissing me softly on my neck and with two fingers of his right hand he massaged my clit till it sent emergency signals to my honey hive to shoot geysers of cum. Oh my gosh! It felt so good to just be naked and have a man touch me like he did. I led him upstairs to the master bedroom. He took off his shirt and I sucked his nipples. I eased him out of his pants and boxers. Then I led him into the bathroom and we both just let the hot water rain down on us. He turned me to face him and started kissing me. Next thing I know, he lifted me as his monty slowly entered me. Slowly thrusting up and down in a steaming hot shower, I started scratching the shower glass. He really knew how to pump it. I jumped off and turned around to the wall. He picked me back up and pulled my hair as his monty re-entered this yoni. His thrusting started speeding and my neck had bite marks like he was Dracula. The more he sped deeper into my walls, the higher my falsetto moans got. The highest note on a piano was the exact same note that blurted out of me every time I came in that round. This was round one. Tyler and I never could just have one sex episode a night. After my anaconda wrapped around his king snake and it exploded ecstasy into my peasant yoni, I jumped off and we just stood there catching our breath not saying a word. I started to bathe him. I rubbed him down from his chest to his monty to his ass to his feet and he did the same to me. The oils were on my shower rack so I told him not to leave yet as I rubbed him down with my vanilla bean oil. He picked the lavender one to rub me down with. We let the water slowly baptize us as we knew raindrops of trapped oil in water would glisten all over us. I stepped out first and grabbed an extra large towel to dry off. As I bent over to dry off my legs, I could sense that he was staring at me. I felt his firm hands go down the crack of my ass and enter me. He was already aroused and ready for round two. I eased back up to stand and stood there as he kept massaging in and out and again. As warm and moist as I was getting, I lifted my leg over the sink while he kissed me between my thighs and started making out with my yoni. I climaxed three times just in that moment. He stopped and I grabbed his hand and walked him over to the bed. I pushed him on his back but he wouldn't let me take charge, not this time. He flipped me over and laid between my legs as his eight inch monty slowly eased into my honey hive, my sweet hydrated yoni until I started constricting his monty like bees swarming and stinging until it swelled inside me. We went two more rounds into the night climax after climax after climax until he fell asleep and I lie gently on his chest. I woke up the next morning feeling great because I got laid but worse because I'm stuck in a situationship I can't seem to get out of due to my feelings being too damn involved. I walked downstairs to make breakfast, nothing fancy, just pancakes, eggs, sausage, and a mini fresh fruit salad (strawberries, blueberries, honeydew, cantaloupe, and grapes). I went back upstairs to wake him but as usual he would never wake up the right way. I slowly eased my warm hands between his thighs and started massaging his monty until the blood flow made it stand at attention. He moaned and opened his eyes and he lifted his head to kiss me.

"Get Up", I said.

"I don't have to be to work for another two hours", he said.

I didn't care if he didn't have to be to work for another thirty minutes, I did not want him in my bed. Granted that we're friends and that's cool and all but mornings is when I need my space. He always dragged around. I guess he never wanted to leave yoni thinking someone was going to get addicted more than him and he would have to strap up. He has always went raw dog no matter what. Since it was him and I knew his sexual history and his emotional state very well, I never pushed the issue.

"If you want breakfast Ty you're going to have to get up."

"I've had breakfast twice this morning" he said. Then he winked at me.

"That is not what I was talking about."

"What's on the menu? He asked.

I replied, "Just some pancakes, scrambled eggs, sausage, and a fresh fruit salad. It's nothing special."

"See, I knew why I always stay over here, you feed me so well," he said.

"I guess I need to hold the food huh?" I replied.

"You know, they say you're supposed to eat dessert earlier in the day because it's healthier for you?" He said.

"I have a meeting with my agent so you're going to have to wait."

He never waits. He just pulled up the t-shirt since that's all I had on at that moment, picked me up and slammed me in slow motion on the bed, and dined between my thighs again making out with yoni till I climaxed twice with notes I never knew I could sing. Damn, he knows exactly when I want it and I never wanted to be dressed. If I could be buck naked, just his muse and he mine whenever our hormones heightened to have sex, I'd be buck naked letting him take all the honey and me swallowing all the dynasties he'd never build. I had to get out the house. After we both went downstairs to eat breakfast, I let him take his shower first. The phone rang. It was my real estate agent. He was helping me look for a location to open up my own poetry café. I had dreamed of owning my own business for years. The money and O.C.D. on locations made it very hard to close on a deal. I heard the water cut off so I ran upstairs to pick out my attire for the meeting then I hopped in the shower after him. After I had finished showering and getting dressed, Ty was trying to go for round three. I knew I had to meet the real estate agent and I couldn't waste anymore time. I just gave up on trying to get him out my house and I just locked up and left. The spot was in Rome, GA that I drove up to. I could already tell that I was going to hate it. I didn't like the location. It wasn't big enough. It needed a lot of repairs before it was ever to be open for business. I immediately told him that this wasn't what I wanted. Pissed that he made me come all of this way for nothing, I just marched to my car and drove off.

Ch. 3

Today I'm just going to get my head right and write for my feature tonight at the Woman, I Am event. I'm very nervous about this event. I heard knocks on the door.

"Who is it?" I said.

"It's your mother, open this door!" She replied.

I opened the door and hugged her.

"Hey mom, I thought you were coming later."

"Well, I decided to come early and surprise my baby." She said.

"I'm not doing anything right now but writing for tonight's event."

"Does that boy still come around here?" She asked.

"Mom!" I yelled.

"Well, I just don't like him coming around all the time. You can't keep giving away the honey especially if he's not going to commit." She said.

"We're just friends" I said.

"Let me tell you about "just friends", those "just friends" will have you just pregnant while they just go on about their business with no responsibility." She said.

"It's not even like that, Mom!"

"You can call it whatever you want to but I know because I'm mom and that boy is going to hurt you to the bone. Guys like that have agendas, mark my words, he wants you as long as he can have you for free." She replied.

"Mom, we're not serious and are not looking to be. I told you we're just friends."

She replied, "I'm going to tell you once more so you young folk can get it, men don't stay friends with pretty girls without going diving into the honey hive. As long as you let him have it, it's going to be real hard to pull away. There's a deep rooted soul tie in all of this that y'all young folk don't understand and that by it self will tear you to pieces."

She kept talking and talking.

"A hard head makes a soft behind. When you get ready to pull away from that man, everything around you will remind you of him to cologne, music, food, movies, and everything else he's touched even that honey hive between your legs every time you get wet, you'll think about him." She kept saying.

I really just let that go in one ear and out the other. I am twenty-eight years old going on twenty-nine and I'm grown enough to make my own decisions in life. I know she means well but I have to learn for myself. Here comes my manager Daniel calling me. Daniel and his identical twin David (my agent) are the sexiest twins in the south. They are definitely about six foot five and high yellow. Trust me I have thought about trying them both but I've never so far.

"Hello" I said.

"What's going on short thang?" He replied.

"I'm just prepping for tonight's event."

"You think you're going to be ready for the crowd tonight?" he asked.

"I don't have a choice now do I?" I replied.

"You can't look at it that way. It will be a great show. What's so nerve wrecking about today that isn't like the others?" He asked.

"For one, my mother is here, not saying she isn't supportive but I have never performed in front of her." I replied.

"There's nothing wrong with that. Your mom just wants to be there to see her baby shine. You're the youngest and the closest child in connection so just breathe and perform like she isn't there," He said.

"That's the thing, she is there," I replied.

"Do you want her to not show up?" He said.

"No!" I said.

I love my mom dearly but I have never performed any of my poetry in front of her. Some of it is too explicit for her. We got off the phone shortly after that and I had to get dressed for the event. I turned on the hot water and started to strip down. All I wanted to do was let the water run down my body and breathe. Mom decided to stay with my sister Yasmine. I heard voices as I was stepping in the shower. You know I had to reach for the first thing in sight and lucky me there was nothing there that would put someone's lights out. The voice sounded familiar as it was coming closer. All of a sudden I remembered that I had given Ty a key to my house after I had passed out six months ago. The voice started getting closer and closer. I heard someone's zipper open and clothes hit the floor. Ty had walked up behind me startling me as I grabbed the plunger.

Ty laughed. "What were you going to do with that?" he asked.

"What do you think? I was going to protect myself" I replied.

"Just don't get any shit juice on my face!" He said.

"Ew, you are so nasty!"

"Give me a kiss" He said.

"You want it, take it!" I replied.

He leaned in for the kiss and immediately I got wetter than Niagara Falls. I pulled away after his tongue made love to mine.

"I have to get ready for my feature event tonight". I said.

"It won't take that long." He whined.

"Now you know you can't just have one round and be over with." I replied.

Before I could even say anything else, Ty had already bent me over and was having a four course meal with yoni like he was dining on a five hundred dollar tab for one. His tongue was digging in deeper into her till my honey flushed him out. A river flooded between my thighs evacuating down his throat. I had to force myself to stop before I would lose all professional merit and be late. I showered with him and let him rub me down with my body wash. The longer he rubbed me down, the harder it was for me to pull away. I had made up my mind and told him to just lie in my bed till I get back or he can go with me. I told him my mom would be there so he just decided to stay in my bed, buck naked. As I was putting on my clothes and doing my hair I could see him from the mirror with his legs spread massaging his monty motioning for me to put it to sleep. I just turned away and began twisting my hair into a halo braid or what some call the milk maid braid. I had on a red sheer dress to my knees and gold stilettos. I walked over to the bed to kiss him and tell him that I'd be back but all he did was whine and moan. I couldn't stand for a man to moan. That was my weakness. I didn't wear panties so I just sat on his monty and rocked him gently back and forth, up and down and again. As I was rocking, I bent forward to kiss him and kept riding him till I squeezed every life out of that monty and watched it flat line. I washed myself down there and checked my hair to make sure it was still okay. I put on my diamond hoops earrings and kissed him while he was sleeping and tiptoed down the stairs and walked out. I drove to the location on Boulevard. It was huge and just the kind of location that I wanted when I opened my own business. I arrived at the location thirty minutes before. Not a good start I told myself. The host had already introduced everyone else and I was last. He introduced me and I walked on stage.

"What's up Atlanta?" I said.

The crowd clapped and yelled back.

"My piece is called "Love the Woman" and I hope you enjoy it as much as I do." I said.

I begin to take a deep breath and close my eyes so I couldn't see my mother.

Love the Woman

"Love me, touch me, you got to love the woman that I am … Sometimes I get weak inside out then again you are my weakness … Are you willing to love the woman that I am? There's no turning back. I might make more money than you but don't let your pride rise and push aside the infinite love between us. I might just need you to hold me. Are you ready to love the woman I am? Love the hot, sweet, wetness of my volcano erupting on your town, drizzling down drowning … burning your forever hard rock mountain. Love the woman I am when I'm quiet and at times listening to the rhythmic beat of your heart matching mine. Identical it becomes… Love the woman I am through the flooded tears to the four day pain to the birthing of a new life to the changing of my last name… Love the woman I am … from the delicacy of my flower to the submissiveness of my service. Love the woman I am from the bubble bath I made you to the tongue massage I gave you. Love the woman I am that knows when we disagree, we will never go to bed on the devil's playground… Love the woman I am pushing forth, writing the covenant we said on our wedding day engraved on your heart. Love the woman I am to know the difference between a cheap jezebel and the queen you see before thee… Love the woman I am that lies beside your sick fragile body with every necessity present to nurse you back to health… Love the woman I am to know that I'm here to encourage your inner man, the hero in you… I'm not the intimidator, the bully, the nagger, the cheater, the heartbreaker, the gold digger, the soul whipper, the heart pimp or the fool to be stepped on. Love the woman I am because I meant every vow I said to you. Love the woman I am through the shadows of my insecurities. Love me! It is time! Can you do it? Can I make you mine? Love the woman I am… Are you ready?"

I stopped speaking and I bowed.

"Thank you Atlanta for having me," I said.

The audience clapped.

The host replied, "Thank you for being here with us. That is all for the show tonight. Let's thank all of the performers. Didn't they do a great job? Well good night and drive safely." Like I always say, "You don't have to go home but you got to get the hell up out of here."

I left the building and went back home hoping that Ty was asleep because I was too tired to do anything. To my answered prayers he was sound asleep, buck naked, and under no covers. He knows he's going to get sick sleeping like that in the cold but he's always told me that my body would warm him up. I undressed and eased in the bed without waking him. Man did I start to crave his naked body and I could hear my mom in my head, "Everything you touch, even that honey hive will get wetter when you think of him. I should have listened because I just wanted to take him in his sleep. I just lied there thinking of all the ways I could just wake him up and fuck. I just eased my hand between my thighs and fell asleep.

Ch. 4

My mom always wanted me to use this platform for the Lord. She said, "God didn't give you that talent to be a ho for the world. You're just being used by a blind druggie". I never told her that I've written just about every genre of poetry. I guess I never wanted her to put me on the spot at her church functions. Don't get me wrong, I was raised in a mixed race church (pentecostal is what they call them) but somehow after college it was out of sight out of mind. I couldn't find a church that reminded me of home but I found new boys that set new memories that home came from between your legs and church was nothing more than a dream your parents forced you to live in. I never felt that way, seeing that I was an overthinker. I guess that's why a lot of things don't go as I plan. Phone rings. Guess who? "Mom" ...

"Hey mom"

"Hey baby, can you do me a favor?" She asked.

I knew we it was coming but I let her say it.

"Can you recite that poem for my 6th Ave on Wednesday night?" She asked.

I didn't know if I could actually do it but I agreed anyway. I knew she could do far worse if I disagreed. Going to mom's church was like going to the gates of heaven. You never knew if you were going to heaven or hell. There were so many cliques and they call themselves a "family" church. I've never felt like family. I never even felt like I belonged. I doubt they'd even like my work but I was doing it for my mom. The pastor came over.

"Hey Christina, I haven't seen you in a while. I've missed you in church." He said.

I highly doubt he'd miss me EVER.

"Hey Pastor Riley! I'm doing fine and I've been on a mission." I said.

"I hope it's a mission for the Lord." He replied.

I always had a comeback one liner on deck.

"Everything is always for the Lord if you let him lead you." I stated.

"Yes, Jesus!" He shouted.

Heading to my seat the praise team began to sing "Not A Slave". Worship songs always made me cry and this one was no different. Then they kept coming with "Since Your Love", "Set A Fire", and "Forever by Bethel Music". Why would they do this to me? Now my make-up is not on point and I look a mess. I ran to the bathroom to fix my face. Two old ladies were talking about how they loved the old hymns and how the church used to be in revival. I used to be that way but-- Nevermind. Revival will always be different each time God steps in. Then my mom walks in the bathroom.

"Are you nervous?" She asked.

"Do I have anything to be nervous about?" I repied.

"Well no"

"Then I'm not nervous."

I really was just ready to get this over with. I fixed my make-up and walked out. I took a seat near the middle side of the church and waited till it was my time to go on. Pastor Riley dapped up those steps like he was pimp walking on the street. Waiting impatiently, I could feel a kid breathing heavily and snorting as my head was down. I looked up to see some snot-nosed kid staring at me with all of the rainbow colored beads knotted down at the end of her braids. This girl looked too damn old to be sucking her thumb. Her parents should have put some good ole' hot sauce on that thing. Poor child will need braces very soon if she doesn't kick the habit. Then I kept hearing a thump. Lord, help me before I beat someone's child today.

I turned around and this curly, sandy brown headed boy with hazel eyes was kicking my seat.

"Boy if you don't cut that out, I will whip you myself." I whispered.

"You not my mama!" He stated.

Oooh, I can't stand kids who are disrespectful to other adults like damn whoop your kids please. Pastor Riley introduced me and as I was walking the little brat hit me. I can't wait to get this over with so I can leave. I slowly walked up the aisle and grabbed the mic. I took a deep breath and began.

"This piece is called "I Wasn't Ready". I hope you like it."

I Wasn't Ready

Time and time over you said you were coming back… no one knows the hour or day. My soul just felt like a castaway… I was not Esther, a humble woman prepared to take on all of the responsibilities. You said you were coming back… you said that the century before this and the century before that… Like a father seemingly making broken promises… I believed you not to be real… can you bill me the check for the spilled blood off your back … I promise to repay you… donate the blood from my heart… I wasn't ready! My life is falling apart. I needed you! Where were you when my head was being bashed in the wall? I wasn't ready! I wasn't perfect… My oil had not been saved. You took your precious time, so I spent it all the way. I took my precious innocence and sold it ten cents a pound… 'Cause you said you were coming back but you were nowhere to be found… I wasn't ready! I had to survive… In and out of jail… weighing havoc on my parents' lives… Lying on my back while they were whipping the life out of yours… I wasn't ready! I thought I had my whole life to enjoy. You said we were in the last days and a false prophet would arise but then there were World War I&II that you let slip by… so yeah I wasn't ready! I had no dress to maintain… I had no oil for my lamp to see your face and those eyes burn like flames… I wasn't ready! I thought you were lying! ... An old wise tale... none of this good book was I applying... I thought I had time to mix and mingle... Going to strip clubs, dropping singles... I wasn't ready! I was impatient. I had so much built up fear. I planned to get my life together. Please don't leave me here! Dark and alone ... I tried to call my mamma but she was already gone. I wasn't ready! I wasn't dressed... Wait! Let me zip up my dress. I didn't think all of those disasters were warning signs... I mean c'mon, don't you think that was a little too much. I wasn't ready! Not right now! My heart wasn't in it but she said and he said ... You know there's no blame on me! I wasn't ready! Give me a minute... Let me search for my things. I found two pennies. Can I give you this offering? Yeah, I know I skipped out on my tithe but there was something I wanted. Yes, I should have trusted you but I was living in the moment. You've got to give a sister a break. An excuse for trying! I wasn't ready! I promise, I thought you were lying. You would have thought by my history I'd finally get it together... The storms kept coming and I couldn't take anymore of this weather. I wasn't ready! If you wait... hold on... take me fifteen minutes ... Let's think, shoes, clothes, make-up, oh and can't forget my daily dose of the good 'ole B-I-B-L-E. I wasn't ready! I promise, just wait right here! If you loved me like you love me you'd wait one more year. Please don't turn your back and act like you don't know me. I wasn't ready! I told you I was sorry. I can't concentrate on that book. I just don't get it. I tossed it aside and never read it. Hold on, where is that verse. What was the last thing you said? I know I learned it in Sunday school. My mamma would quote it every day. I get tired of this quoting so I turned a deaf ear, put you on the back burner, and left my wedding ring right here. Wait! Where did it go? Oh, I sold it on Ebay. My bills had to get paid. Please wait! Don't go! I wasn't ready, I promise! You said you'd forgive me. Where is the truth in that? I told you I wasn't ready! On the table was his wedding ring as he wiped away the tear. He said I never knew you, but I thought I had a year.

I bowed. The congregation clapped. I went back to my seat.

Ch. 5

There were so many other performers. Some boring, some funny, and some well let's just say never should perform again. When the service was over I left. Heading down 65 southbound I took exit 259 towards University Blvd and took the scenic route to my house near the Vulcan on top of the hill. I don't know why I chose to live on a hill but the house was too beautiful to pass up. Seeing bikers ride up and down the inclined hill to prep for their marathons was nice. If I wouldn't have quit trying then maybe I would have been able to ride a bike. Pulling up in my garage, I noticed that Ty's cobalt blue Lexus was already parked in front of the house. I had the semicircle drive around as well. He opened the door and stepped out in a cashmere button down with the Perry Ellis pants and the penny loafers. I loved a man that could dress. One thing I really loved about him was the way he carried himself. I never had to worry about him tripping over his pants half down his ass. He waited as I got to the door. I opened the door and walked in and he closed it behind me.

"How was your day?" He asked.

"It was good enough"

"Did the pastor preach a good sermon?"

Now he knows I hate small talk. The minute I bent over to take my shoes off, I knew I didn't even have to answer that question. He was already on his knees, pulling my panties to the side, and hydrating his dehydrated tongue as it vibrated against my clitoris. I never could bend over in front of him. He's always in heat like a dog to everything. His tongue kept it's circular motion slowly then he slid his middle and pointer finger in my pussy. Wet as the ocean, he kept pounding it in and out while keeping his rhythm of his tongue trying to over hydrate himself on my clitoris. The more he moved, the closer I got to climax. Falsettos was all I could ever speak.

"Ooooooooooh shit!" I screamed.

My legs began to shake and he kept on. It felt like I was being tortured by his tongue. Then I turned around and pulled out his dick. He was hard as hell. I climbed on top of him and I rode him like a frog, sideways, reverse cowgirl, like a helicopter, then like a mechanical bull until his dick exploded inside me. We both laid there on the floor drained and eventually fell asleep naked with him still inside me. I tell you, leaving him is always the hardest. He's so cute when he's sleeping. I just have no idea what I'm going to do when I finally snap out of it. When I woke up, it was already 6pm and dark outside. He was still sleep and I didn't want to wake him but I did it anyway. I told him to go to the bedroom. I walked his sweat glistening, half sleep self upstairs to my room and eased him in the bed. Laying naked, he curled in fetal position and fell back asleep. I've always had a habit of massaging his scalp with one hand and rubbing his behind with the other. He told me to never stop so it's like our routine now. When he finally was fully sleep, I went back down stairs and cleaned house. I took out the trash from the kitchen and my office which was on the other side of the fireplace. Then I washed up dishes from breakfast and began to order in Chinese. He always got the lo mein and I the jumbo egg rolls and the honey or kung pao chicken. The doorbell rang. I went back into the room, got the money out of my purse, went back downstairs and we exchanged food for money. I told him to have a blessed day before shutting the door and laying the food on the coffee table. Ty was up there sleeping peacefully and I didn't want to wake him. I turned on the t.v. and switched to a rerun of A Different World. It was the episode where Gina was in an abusive relationship. I loved that show. The 90s were good for blacks in television. I opened my food and began to eat. Trying not to yell too loud but I was still arguing at the t.v. as if they could hear what I was saying. It gets worse watching Lifetime. When I was almost done with my food, Ty woke up and walked downstairs.

"I see you're up now." I said.

"Yeah, what's for dinner?" He asked.

"I ordered Chinese." I replied.

I patted the seat motioning for him to sit next to me. I could tell he was still sleepy. Ty is a big baby when he's either sleepy or sick. Something didn't feel right. He always went straight for the food when he wakes up or he just goes for round two. This time, all he did was lay his head in my lap. I felt his forehead and he was hot. I made him sit up. I was trying to take his shirt off.

"I'm not in the mood right now"

"Look boy, you're burning up. If you had less clothes on maybe your body could cool off."

Then he let me proceed in taking his shirt off. He laid his head back in my lap. I told him to get up. I went upstairs to my room and got my inner ear thermometer. I checked his temperature while he laid in my lap and it read 102 even. I knew something was going on. He wasn't like that when he got here. At least he didn't tell me he was sick. I escorted him back to the bed. He took off his boxers and laid on top of the covers. Then it all started coming. He ran to the bathroom and dropped to the floor. He was coming out of both ends. Head was in the toilet vomiting while he was bent over shitting on my floor ugh. I was so pissed that he crapped on my floor but felt bad for him that he was this sick. I double gloved and put a mask on. I got a dirty old pink towel and cleaned my floor. He kept throwing up in the toilet. I grabbed the whole full roll of toilet paper and started tearing off several sheets at a time and wiping his butt. I knew he was finished for now when he just scooted over to the space in front of the sink and laid there. I had to get him cleaned up so I ran some water and helped him get in the shower. Bending over was making him nauseous so I just washed him down then dried him off and eased him back in bed. I laid beside him to watch him for a few minutes. Then he rolled over on top of me more like between my legs, lifted my shirt, pulled my boobs out my bra, grabbed hold of them and fell asleep. I was pretty much stuck there. What do you do in my situation? You call your friend to clean up downstairs and lunch is on you next time. I had to call and cancel my appearance tonight at the theatre. Phone rings. Brittani was calling. She was pulling up in the driveway. Britt and I met in second grade at recess. She was the "ride or die" best friend that anyone would want to have. She beat up this one bully I had. That girl never messed with me again.

"Hey Britt Bratt?"

"Sup, so you want me to do what?"

"Just put the food sitting on the coffee table in the fridge and tidy up."

Now I know she wants to know why I called her all the way over to clean up.

"Why can't loverboy clean up downstairs? Don't you feed him enough?" She asked.

"Well F.Y.I., Ty is sick." I replied.

"He can't be that sick."

"Ty has a 102 fever and I just cloroxed my whole bathroom because he was throwing up and shitting at the same time. He's that sick."

"Oh, well I'm downstairs. I got a lot to tell you."

"It's going to have to be over lunch tomorrow because Ty is knocked out and I can't move."

"Well you go on and be Ms. Love Doctor then."

"I'll see you tomorrow okay."

"I'm picking the restaurant and the most expensive thing on the menu"

"I don't have it like that now. One day it will be a "you can have whatever you like" but nope"

"Well, I just put up everything and I'm headed out to cram for this exam."

Brittany was in med school about to finish out.

"Thanks again"

"You owe me"

"That I do"

She left and we hung up. I knew that I could be Ty's wife someday. It felt good to take care of a sick adult. My feelings for him were starting to show. I knew that we couldn't hide behind the "just friends" line anymore. By the time I tried to stay woke to watch him, I was getting sleepy. I fell asleep in whatever I had on. Which wasn't much, just an oversized tee.

Ch. 6

I woke up and it was like two in the morning. Ty was laying next to me with his head facing the other way. I reached over and checked his forehead and it felt clammy like he was sweating in his sleep. I turned over and got my thermometer out my night stand and checked his temperature and it was 98.6 so I thanked God that that whatever that was had passed. I threw away that clip and headed to the bathroom. Finally, I was able to have some alone time. I flushed and washed my hands, grabbed a towel and dried them and went back to bed. Time I pulled the covers over me, Ty was awake and all over me. I was not in the mood. All I wanted to do was go back to sleep so I can be alert in the morning for my meeting with the twins. I was still trying to find this building for the café. Ty was not having that. It was time for round three for him.

"Ty, go back to sleep! I have to get up in the morning and so do you."

I never understood why he all of a sudden never wanted to sleep in his own place. I had been to his place several times. We have a key to each other's houses, but he seems to use mine the most.

"I know that but I feel better now. I want to thank you for staying with me."

"Thank me?! You can thank me by rolling your ass over and going back to sleep!"

Ty knew EVERYTHING about my body. He knew how to turn me on and how to push the envelope to be satisfied. He started to ease his hands between my thighs from behind. Massaging her like "Wash on, wash off". I couldn't do a thing but spread my legs wider. He said he wanted to thank me so he started kissing every imperfection on my body then down my stomach and then lower to my pelvis then center to her. It felt so good. He kept kissing and licking it as he lifted my legs high in the air. The more he licked in a circular motion, the more my body squirmed till my legs shaked. I belted out

"Shit! Why?! Ahhh"

This fool kept licking even after that. He was not stopping. It was like the hunger games and my yoni was the first mission. His tongue was the first weapon. He then pushed the sheets back and slid inside. OMG! It was so deep I think he cracked my diaphragm. He was long stroking it. Then he pulled out, stood up on the floor picked me up, spread my cheeks and slammed me down on his dick. In the air we tore that bedroom up just air squats and upside down spinning. I was bouncing it on his dick until he had my head in the space between the wooden sleigh bed headboard and the mattress. I knew I was stuck and it was game on. Face down, ass up and he was ready to tear it up. Fast pounding like he was the lead actor in Crank. Toes began to curl. Back was nicely arched. He was pounding and smacking that ass like I was a bad ass kid.

"Damn! Don't stop! Ugh ugh uhhh! Fuck!"

"You coming?!"

"Mmmm yeah, don't stop! Faster! Faster!"

"Baby, what's my name?"

"Tyyyyy! Ahhhhh shiiiiiit!"

"Hold on baby, I'm coming'"

"Aaahhh fuck me deeper!"

It was everthing. We both came one after the other then I hit the shower and went back to bed and fell asleep. He showered too then fell back asleep.

Ch. 7

I woke up and Ty was already gone to work. I put on my clothes already laid out and headed out the door. I had to leave early because I have to take I-20/59 then take 280 to get to the twins' offices. Both of those is a pain in my behind. Like seriously, no one wants to let you over. Tricks want to get over in front of you knowing too damn well they see you in the next lane. Traffic stay backed up because someone always wrecks.

"Ugh! Go! I got places to go man!"

I swear these people can't drive down here. They either scared to or they like this fool in this black sedan with the windows rolled down.

I blew my horn.

"Move the fuck on and stop applying your make-up to your cracked face!"

She probably broke that mirror anyway because she had one of those wall mirrors in her lap not paying attention to the road.

I was so happy to take the next exit and find a parking space where their office is. Their building was about seven stories and they were the whole 6th floor. When I got out the car and locked it, I pulled out my badge showing that I was a client and walked up and swiped my I.D. card. The doors unlocked and I walked in. I took the elevators instead of the stairs because I was already sore from earlier with Ty. Man that elevator stunk so bad. It smelled like ass, skunk, burnt eggs, pneumonia pee, and shit. I mean do these people not know what soap is. Every time I come here something always stinks when I get here but when I leave it's fresh. Keep that Lysol and Airwick aerosol spray in my purse too. I can't take any chances when they violate my senses. Finally, I reach my floor and took the first right then the fourth door on the left. Somehow they still liked to share things. They share offices like they don't want to be pulled apart. It's not really my business though. I walked in their office and caught them nodding.

"Good morning!" I said.

"Hey, I see you didn't get lost this time", Daniel said.

"How many people did you curse out on the drive here?" David asked.

"Not that many Dave, but I swear if y'all don't do something about who ever is stinking up this whole facility with their body odor, I will."

"What are you going to do?" Daniel asked."

"I'm going to kindly scope this place out or just tell everyone to give their clients some soap as a gift. Something!"

"You know we can't do that." David said.

"Y'all need to do something. I can't keep having this smell rape my senses every time I come here."

"We'll think of something." Daniel said.

"Back to the matter at hand, have you found a place for your commercial business? Time is ticking." David asked.

"No, not really. Ty gave me a spot on 1st Ave N that I want to check out. Another is in Brookwood that I seen. Then there is one in the summit area that I want to check out as well."

"Ty is still sticking around huh?" David asked.

"Yes, why you ask?"

"Ty from the 404, ATL, the well--, I just don't like him as a suit for you." David stated.

"That is my business, my decision."

"Basically, at the moment, he's giving you the business?" Daniel asked.

"Like I said, it's my business."

"You know we're just trying to look out for you. Anyway, you know I had to find another event since you cancelled last minute last night."

Yeah I know Dan. Long story and I apologize but in my calendar the next event is on a campus?

"Yeah, Miles College wants you there for an open mic. All you have to do is open it up then introduce the other artists." Daniel stated.

Sometimes I liked going on campuses and sometimes I hated it. College was good and bad for me. I met half of my friends there. I'm glad it ended right at eleven this time. My friend chose the Macaroni Grill. I thought it was Britt and I but it ended up being Britt, Sara, Natalie, Jennifer, and I. We was seated by this fine brother in college named Miguel. It all made us go down memory lane.

"Hey guys"

We took a booth.

Brittani and I sat beside each other. I always had the outside seat and Sara and Jennifer sat beside each other. Natalie sat between Sara and Brittani.

"How's everyone doing lately?" Britt asked.

"I am drowning in all of this studying for nurse practitioner school." Natalie said.

Oh Natalie! Natalie was the soft spoken one. I met her my sophomore year in college taking a behavioral health class.

"Well you'll get through this. How many more semesters?"

"Last one and I'm done." Natalie said.

"You can do it Nat!" Britt said.

"How about you Sara?"

Sara and I met in the second grade as well. Her parents died when she got into high school so my parents became her legal guardians. Sara's had it rough. I guess coming home to your whole life ending in front of you can mess you up psychologically. I was trying to get out of the counseling roll and be "Christina, the writer".

"My day has been good so far. I can't speak for the previous days."

"What's going on Sara?" Britt asked.

"I caught Thomas cheating with two other women. I mean to see the man you love, your husband and the father of your kids just going at it like that disgusts me."

"How did you catch him? Jennifer asked.

Jennifer was always trying to get everyone to spill all of the tea. I mean she thirsts for every detail of drama. I met Jennifer my freshman year of college and knew something was not right in the head with this girl. Sara spilled it was all I can say and I mean she told it all.

"I was coming home from twelve hours of work and was still on call from Children's but I thought we could get it on since the kids were at grandma's. She said.

She let her kids call my parents grandma but I didn't care. She had no other family.

"I took off my coat and shoes at the door and walked over to the bedroom. I noticed the door was cracked. I'm looking in through the crack and he had the audacity to be butt naked with these hoes. One girl was riding his face and the other was riding his dick."

The food came and we were all tuned in like it was a "Waiting to Exhale" series.

"I froze. I couldn't do a damn thing." I didn't know whether to be pissed or join."

"Join?!" Jennifer said with that side eye.

"Look I didn't participate. I just stood there. Like two fat ass women were slobbing the knob. I mean why my man? How long was this going on? I stood there like a fool watching him lick each one of those pussies and kiss both of them. Watched them kiss each other and wonder where the hell is my sanity and why didn't I do something?"

"I'm pissed just listening, so what did you do?" Britt asked.

"I kept still and watched him get his gspot licked by one ho while he kept licking the other ho's pussy. I'm stupid for standing there like I was a drone on pause. He looked so good naked. Why was he fucking these hoes? I finally got fed up watching."

I would have been fed up once I seen it but not my life.

"I bust open that door and looked at him"

"What the hell Thomas?!"

"It's not what you think, I don't love them. I was just helping them." Thomas stated.

"Helping them do what? It seemed like you were fucking two hoes and got caught."

"Then this fool asked me could I join them."

"Hell no!" Sara said.

Thomas was a crook and I don't see how she got mixed up with him. She met him in a club when we were in college.

"He stood up butt naked then and dragged me over there. He ripped off my scrubs and all and tossed me on the bed. He told me to get on all fours. My ass was out and he spread my lips and let hoe number one lick me while hoe number two sucked my breast. I felt violated but I really wanted my husband."

I knew for sure we were going to get thrown out with her life story. I think the whole section was waiting for her to finish because half of them paid and no one left.

"Then he pushed the girls head away and had her on all fours beside me. He was eating my pussy and massaging hers with his hand. Then he violently started fucking me like I was in the wrong for catching him in the act. He pulled out his gun as one of the girls tried to leave and told her to get her ass back on the bed. We're all naked and I was mad at myself for lowering my standards. I wanted to kill him after those hoes left. I didn't. I just laid there and fell back asleep to his naked ass and hoped the next day he wouldn't beat me to it." Sara said.

"Well my day is going great. Even though no one has asked all lunch." Jennifer interrupted.

We finished the food and had ordered drinks. Jennifer just liked the beers. Sara got whatever margarita she could get. I ordered the red wine and Britt doesn't drink. We sat there and cracked jokes about the other customers, took pictures with our waiter, and posted them on Instagram. It seemed like when we got older, technology got better for itself and worse for us. We began stealing from the family setting to post it online. Too many of us, and I am guilty of it, are in a hypnotized state, eyes glued to the phone and not in tune with life itself. My mother always said if the Lord ever came back, most of us would be too busy worshipping our phones that we wouldn't even know that he came and left until someone close to us is no longer here. I don't know about that but it kind of makes sense I guess. After we had enough drinks, we all left to go home or wherever we had to go. We always ended with kisses on each cheek. I headed home to relax just in case Ty decided to crash at my place. I called my mom because that story Sara told us at lunch was not settling with me. I knew he had beaten her again. Sara tells just enough to let you get the crazy part but won't tell you the "I almost died" moments. She never tells me but I already know and with one look, she confesses. The phone rings twice before she picks up.

"Hey Tina."

"Hey mom, how's everything going?"

"Everything is going well. I'm just a little tired but I'm fine."

"You sure? I can't afford to "almost" lose you again."

"Hush with all of that! I'm not going anywhere. Have you found a place yet?"

"No ma'am. I'm going out to three locations later in the week to scope them out per se."

"Have you talked to Sara?" I had her kids two weeks ago and we had so much fun. You know, I worry about that child."

"I know you do mama. All of the girls and I had lunch. Well Sara decided that she was going to tell the details of everything. I felt embarrassed that she was that open and in a restaurant full of strangers. Trust me mama, I don't have a good feeling about her staying in this toxic marriage."

"Well child, you know some people want love so bad that they will settle for lust even if it's dressed in Hell just to taste the water of heaven."

"You lost me there."

"Sara doesn't have a direction to go to after her parents died. She's trying to find what could have been her father's love if he was living by staying in this relationship. It's her comfort but also her Titanic. The titanic was good before it hit that hard spot and sunk. If she's not careful everything surrounding that ship will die along with it."

Mom always had a way with her words. She made perfect sense. I want to save my friend like old times but I just don't know how. I don't know if I can anymore. She won't leave. She's been kicked out of the House of Ruth in different states because she kept going back. She's sincerely a caged bird that doesn't know that door is open and she can fly now. I really want to see her fly. I fear she'll never get that chance.

Ch. 8

Night came and it was time to perform at the college. The wardrobe now has gotten insanely out of hand. Now men don't wear their pants on their hips. Not only do they sag but they sag in tight skinny jeans or jeggings as if their manhood already wasn't violated by the big baggy pants with their boxers hanging out in the 90s- early '00. They had me in their history building. I was nervous as usual. Miles was mostly black but I still went because I was getting paid to speak. They introduced me and I calmly walked to the podium, heart racing, heavily breathing, closed my eyes and went for it.

Speaks For Itself

You know, bold young Malala standing proud for her rights in a country where women are taught to be docile and totally submissive. I think of a girl her age here who wouldn't even pick her voice up off the floor because get this "That's not her problem". When did our history become just our past and "Not our problem" was our pitch line as if we didn't care. Seem more interested in new shoes and stolen hair … Stolen from an innocent child across the seas while we break the innocence of ours molding and relaxing their identity. Wigs and fake nails, tight dresses and high heels, but while we're training our babies to be exactly what the black market want … another lost child sold as a slave to the lust of a man with explicit thoughts. Now I'm thinking of the son being drugged from his home as they set his parents on fire, weeping in the night… they turn him into a man…

put a gun in his hand and said shoot them... I come to my country and see a boy 'bout his age, pants sagging as if he were telling the "gay nation", come get it... I don't want education... that sh— is for the birds... while you're sleeping on your enemy ... doesn't matter your voice won't be heard. Then it takes me back to a pain staking story of how a little girl of thirteen was stitched up sixteen times her glory... no sedative... just screaming... "we want you to stay a virgin" they say... I know not to lie down so why stitch it up anyway... I don't get why my young sisters are so easy to explore... when the only thing you're after walks in and out of your front door... I think of this crazy terror of toddlers... my nieces gassed to ash... I weep and morn for their future is long gone... Say, what about our children who were gunned down on our land and no there is no difference... the weapon always runs to the psycho's hands... How they spilled their own descents blood on a cold cement while everyone got their turn to walk on it... Brings me back to the same spilled heritage, spilled identity they gunned down in Darfur, Rhowanda... Hell any third world country ... and tell me is our land more important ... is hunger and rape more important in this country because our home is not overseas so their struggle has got to be dead to me... Well, maybe not dead, just fallen on deaf ears, dry tears, twenty years and no break for the broken... No break for my ancestors who lost their innocence... blood shed on mother nature's dark black dirt... her dark brown skirt... writing years of torture like the scarlet letter of shame she would always wear... reminding her if a land stolen... it took broke backs to get her walking down a weary trail of tears over two hundred years and there's still no sorry. Well, if it wasn't said then... then save it! I don't need your sorry for the pain we endured. Not like it's going to help while the past they're trying to conjure... bring it back ... so we can as they say, "Be put in our place"... throw the last fifty years of progression back in our face. The ill racism of the past is still the racism of today. Don't let them trick you into thinking that we are all post racism... sitting at the dining table singing Kumbaya... like snakes weren't crawling in your Boudreaux. History speaks for itself and there's no need to tell it. Let your voice be your sword and your blood run through ... your blood's the same as somebody's ... not we bleed the same blood too?

I took a bow when that was all over. I stayed around for questions. The Q/A wasn't so intense this time around. One time I spoke at Howard University and it was so intense in the room, you wished we all had oxygen tanks just to revive ourselves. Coming from Miles, I stopped at the Walmart on Lakeshore Dr. to get a few items for the house. I promise you, never go there late at night. It becomes club Walmart. No one has any time to be putting up with women wearing club dresses with the sides cut out with boxcar bodies. I don't care to see dresses so short that every time they bend down you can see the inside of their vaginas. I just hate it. I got in there and got out quickly and headed home. I hated driving uphill but I was glad to be back at home. I unlocked the door and locked it back. Thank God that Ty wasn't here tonight. He had to go out of town on business for two weeks. I put the items away and headed upstairs to shower. After that, I laid across the bed and turned on the television. The news was still on. I changed it to CNN and there was another shooting of an unarmed teenager. The officer feared for his life supposedly but the teen looked like the whimpy kid on that movie. The cop looked like he had a side hustle body building. Some times I wonder how many dummies have been let on the force. I feel that if a person has been reprimanded in the last 5-10 years and/or could not pass a psych/behavioral evaluation then they should not be put on the force. I'm just tired of the same storyline just different person. I guess I'll be tuned in all night to see how this spins.

Ch. 9

I stayed up all night too watching the news. I hate when the media tries to depict us in a bad limelight. It's like our past is now the first thing that comes up. A person's past should not be put out there like they're on trial. I mean it was a kid. This was someone's child who everyone is talking about in a negative way because he is dead. I guess the saying is true that your secrets or past comes out worst when you die. You really start to see how others see you. Not that you would see anything being six feet under and all. I was so pissed at the fact of this and they sprayed sixteen bullets in this child and watched him die. He was still alive and they stood over him while he died. They say they have new evidence of a video. I can't wait to see how this spins as well. I finally went to bed at three a.m. and I must have been really tired because I didn't hear my alarm go off at all. I was supposed to be up two hours before my next speaking engagement for black history month. I guess I'll just have to rush myself in this little time limit. Daniel had called me three times by the time I turned my phone on. I heard a knock on my door and he was all dressed.

"Good Morning sunshine"

I'm just one of those people you give caffeine to first before you address me.

"Yeah"

"We were suppose to be on the road already. Did you forget?" Daniel asked.

"No, I didn't forget. I was just up all night writing my next piece and I turned to the news and was staying on top of that kid who got shot up north."

"Yeah, I heard about that. We have to stay woke on situations like these. We have to be active at all times from marches to petitions to speaking out."

"Yes, true"

Now I know He has more paragraphs coming out of his mouth, but I had to rush an hour's worth of getting ready into fifteen minutes. This is not the time for me to engage in any productive, pro-black conversations. Hell, I was still sleepy. I wish I could just crawl back into my bed and go back to sleep but my schedule won't allow that at the moment. Hell, my schedule won't allow me to sleep for this whole year. I am booked, overbooked, stretched out. You name it. My name is on it. I finally got finished and got in the car. The driver drove us to Atlanta. Don't ask me to know where the hell I'm going because I am not a roadie. I just get in and drive and/or ride (sleep). After what seemed like a long ride which it was only a little over an hour, we arrive at the ILounge on Glenwood Ave. Nice place here. I was looking at their interior and dreaming of my own place. Once the other poets came in, we began the history of our ancestors and then everyone started smoking the microphone. One guy in his lapel suit was talking about the school to prison pipeline. Another poet was talking about the parallels between killing our own kind and other races killing us. My favorite was a small girl who talked about the horrors of hanging and how it would be if it were reversed. That one was powerful. It was my turn and like always I got nervous. This was one of my earlier works and I didn't want anyone to look at it as less than. I've always been transparent about my feelings and how others see me as a writer compared to others. To avoid looking at the other poets who were not my competition, I closed my eyes and let it rip.

"This is to all my people going through pain in this racially divided country"

Am I Less Than?

I am my own person… I didn't choose the skin I'm in… does that male me less than?! History, fashion, music has changed… just because I love where it has arrived, does that make me less than? I was born in an era where a grandfather clause does not exist… I am strong willed and anything unjust I will resist… Does that make me less than? I married someone from your skin. Does that make me less than? I wear what is comfortable to me or professional to me, but do how I look threaten you? Does that make me less than? My hair is curly and kinky… my mind might be also but does what I act on make me less than? I am different! I am powerful! I am bold and I am the truth! Does this bullet called my tongue shooting back at you make me less of an American, less of a human, or less of a woman? I came from a diverse background and I don't agree on everything you say or do. I'm not a yes massa slave to you. Does that make me less than? I am the secret you cannot hide, the shed blood you cannot lose… the truth you cover as a lie staring you dead in your face… Does that make me less than? I turn my music and I sing and dance to it. I can get wild and who's to say I wasn't as a child. Does that make me less than? Am I less than? I am not! I am the lie you cover… the truth you hide… I am the mirror of my ancestors reminding you of your sins. I am the voice of my people and the vote to get you out. I will not lay down my mouth for a dead man can't count. Am I less than?! I am not! My life is more than your guilty account. Don't think of me as less than. As my goliath, I'll knock you down. I am never less than! Let my mouth be the sword to cut you up and spit you out.

I was so happy that this was over. We got in the car and hit the road so fast. I was glad we didn't get stopped by a cop. I was so glad to see my bed. All alone again at last.

Ch. 10

It had been two weeks since I seen Ty. I was knocked out when he came in. I woke up and he was "the usual" in my bed. His arm was wrapped around me with his hand under my shirt gripping one breast. I noticed and fell back asleep. I didn't care that he never went straight home. I was so drained that I knew something was wrong. I remembered later that "red bull" was on it's way. I never understood where these old women got these names for your cycle from but each generation still adopted them and still uses those names. My fatigue was on an all time high. I didn't want to do anything. If I called home, I knew my mom would tell me to slow down then take some vitamin B12 and some iron pills to make sure my body had enough iron so during blood loss I wouldn't be too tired. I'm not a pill popper so yeah I just skip those advices. By the time it finally came on, I was snappy. Ty knew not to be around me but I can never seem to get him to leave. He stays there like a sad, sick puppy. Thank God it's only for three days and then it's over.

"Ty how was your trip?" I asked.

"It was okay. I got to see Johnson while I was there."

"The all-star power forward from college?"

"That's the one"

"How's he doing?"

"I guess he's fine. You know men don't talk like that."

"It's just a simple "how have you been?""

"Again, we don't go into details like women do."

"Stop the lying! Men are the biggest gossipers I know."

"I beg to differ."

"We'll just agree to disagree because I could hurt your little feelings if I wanted to."

"Seriously?!"

"Yes"

Tyler thinks he knows everything but men gossip the worst hence the barbershop chronicles. They will sit up and tell every detail just like a woman in a hair salon. Sometimes men get their rocks off by snitching a few secrets too just to see how you'd react. I was glad that Ty had to go to work in the morning. He was in sports medicine so he travels. It looks like we see each other a lot from the outside looking in but it really is the exact opposite. I mean it shouldn't bother me when he's gone for a long time. We're just friends. At least that's what I keep force feeding myself with. That friendship is something way more. It's on a train at full speed and I can't seem to slow it down. My mother's words kept eating at my ears every time. I really want more from him but I'm not going to pressure him like half of these women do then end up in divorce in less than a year. I know too much about him and vice versa. I just wish I knew verbally how he felt. I already know by actions but it wouldn't hurt to know verbally. I've been reading the "5 Love Languages" book and my love language is definitely quality time but I do need that words of affirmation as well. I'm not a gifts person so that doesn't bother me. I'm not into the acts of service either because I can do it myself. I have to get up off this bed. I have to meet with David today because he is now my lawyer and I have to look over some documents for this real estate then meet up with Daniel about some audition that he set up. Man this mess is taking my strength. I mean I am stuck and not in a good way. Like every time I get up there's a sharp pain. Something has to get cancelled or moved to another date. I called David to cancel. The phone rang three times.

"Good morning Tina"

"Hey, I'm going to have to reschedule that meeting today. I can barely get out of bed."

"What's wrong?"

"You don't want to know"

"From that sentence alone I already do."

"I see you've been around me too long huh?"

"If third grade till now is too long then pretty much."

"What papers did we need to go over?"

"Well we needed to discuss getting the commercial licence now while you're still searching for the building. We can go over all of that when you know ... Uh ... Just call me later."

"Okay, talk to you soon."

I tell you, getting a commercial license is a bore but it is well worth it in the end. I mean you have to get the license, find the place, rent or buy the place, get the permits for the place (alcohol etc.), employees, liability or health insurance. I could just drown myself in all of this paperwork but not today Satan! I called Daniel to find out about this audition that he has set up for me and where it will be held. Daniel mostly answers on first ring.

"Hey Dan"

"Hey, I'm on the other line. Hold on a minute and let me get finished with them."

Dan could talk for a long time. He's known to keep you on hold so long that your arms get heavy and you eventually hang up.

"Hey I'm back, what can I do for you Christina?"

"You called me three times earlier about some audition that you booked for me. What's going on?"

"Yeah, well you know Gene Altman is going to be in Atlanta holding auditions for her upcoming film "No Chains". I knew that she was one of your favorite directors and what better way to break into the film industry than to be apart of her film."

Gene Altman was the Ava Duverney, the Debbie Allen of my generation. She has directed many historical movies like "I Stand By My Word" and "Freedom Comes" to name a few. "Freedom Comes" has won an Oscar, Grammy, Golden Globe, NAACP Image Award and countless others. I don't know how he pulled this off but like my mom tends to say, that was nothing but God. Everything doesn't need to be explained.

"How did you get this?"

I really just wanted to know even though I could hear my mom's voice saying "Trust God" but I had to be nosey.

"I'm not getting in to all of that but the audition is a month out so you have plenty of time to practice. You can either do an original monologue or use one from one of her films."

"I guess I'll have more homework to do."

I thought by getting out of psychology two years ago that I would be able to relax on all of this paperwork. Following my dreams was the best thing I have ever done and I don't regret a thing but it is a sacrifice to everything including my bank account.

"I guess you better hop to it." He said.

Ch. 11

I got off the phone with with Daniel and started to write. As I was trying to get my thoughts together, I turned on the news to catch up on the teen shot up north. It wasn't looking good at all. People were looting their own neighborhoods out of frustration. Why loot from your own people's businesses? The media only covered the looting. They never showed the peaceful marches or the sit-ins. Next month was the 50th anniversary for the March on Selma. I was going no matter what. You know you're mad when you start talking to the television. Those people can't hear a word that I'm saying.

"Why are you looting your own businesses?"

Look at them just burning down the very institutions that they need in their communities like the free clinic and the pharmacy. What good is it to commit arson to those institutions when you know they are the only institutions in your community for a long mile? I just don't understand the stupidity of some people. The ignorant do the crime and the ones that need it the most suffer over time. I'm just listening to them bring out guests and it just pisses me off so much. They're profiling this innocent child like his past has anything to do with his present. All he was doing was walking home from his friend's house and someone thought he looked suspicious so they called the cops and the cops arrived and shot him then watched him die. Weeks later they came back with a not guilty verdict for murder one or two. They basically just got a slap on the wrist. They knew what they did. Their chief put them on administrative paid leave. They'll come back to work and the same shit will keep happening.

Our communities have to stick together in order to see change. There need not be any divide between any of us because it makes a bigger divide between all of us. Three days passed and this thing had finally ended for the month. I wanted to surprise Ty with a little T.L.C. so I got dressed and headed to his place. Ty had this thing that when he needed me it was on his time sometimes. I headed to Trussville off of I20/59 and went around the mountain or curve, whatever. I had a key to his place as well so I unlocked his door and walked in. He wasn't home yet so I checked his cabinets and fridge to see what I could make for him. Well I guess I could start with a chef salad, then a coconut moonshine chicken on a bed of buttered rice with steamed squash. Ty loved coconuts so why not cut out a coconut and make a coconut infused moonshine margarita in a coconut shell. I had the house smelling so good. When Ty walked in, all he could smell was the taste of island. I had the nature instrumental of the waves playing in the background. I am very creative. Well I'd like to think that I am.

"Food smells good in here Tina."

"I tried to do a little something something."

"I had a long day and I am starving."

I yelled out from the kitchen. "Go shower before you come in here."

Ty didn't know what I had in store for him but he sure was about to find out. I've timed him plenty of times and it usually takes him roughly ten minutes in the shower unless he had to use the bathroom then he'd shower again. When Ty came out the bathroom and into the kitchen in his towel, I knew he was trying to sneak up on me but I had a plan. I had already dropped the wrapped coat and was standing in nothing but red pumps. I had already plated the food and had the candles lit on the table. All he had to do was eat. We blessed the food and started eating. The more we ate, the more we were getting hot just staring across the table at each other. Playing feet wars under the table was just the trick to put me over the edge. Right when we were suppose to get it on like we used to, his phone rings.

"Yeah, I did that already. I already told him to relax that knee. Who signed off on this? He was my patient. I never signed off on this."

He was getting heated to the point that he was cursing out whoever was on the other end of that call. The phone call lasted longer than my sleep pattern. I gathered the food, slipped out of my pumps, took the dishes into the kitchen, cleaned up the kitchen, and walked back to the table. When he got off the phone, he was livid. I tried to give him his space for a minute to see what he was going to do. I was already turned off and was grabbing my shoes and coat to leave.

"Where are you going?"

Ty grabbed me and started to reel me in closer. Kissing my neck like he was marking his territory with a hundred hickies. I pushed away.

"I got to get home. It's late"

"I thought you were going to sleep over here tonight."

Trying to slide his fingers between my legs. My pupils could tell you my whole life story in just that one glance staring into his eyes. The look that says I need you so much. Don't stop even if I ask you to. I pushed away again.

"It's late and I have a meeting in the morning."

I knew he was upset but his frustration escalated to an all time high for me.

"Go on then! Get your shit and get out my house. You always get what you want. You never do anything that I want."

"How do I always get what I want? When have I never given you what you wanted?"

"Man go on with that shit! Don't call me, text me, or anything."

I put my coat on and left his house. I sped home. I don't know what his problem was but taking it out on me was the last thing he needed to do. I have put my all into this-- this-- whatever the hell this is.

Ch. 12

I was so pissed when I got home that I thought real hard about changing the locks to my door. I knew I'd never go through with it. Somehow we all have our flaws. Sara's is confusing abuse with a sign for love. Jennifer's is thinking gifts is the sign for love. Natalie hasn't found love. Britt's broken marriage was over way before she said "I do". This thing that I'm in seems to be some kind of sign that a father's love is always needed in a person. My real father isn't here to do that. My pops (step-dad) raised me. I thank him for the woman that I am now but I often wonder what if I had the opportunity to be raised by my father. Would it really be a whole lot different? Would I be a better adult or a criminal? The next morning I had to prep because one of my friend's sister wanted me to speak to her class and do one of my works. I chose "Tap Dance With the Serpent" because it paralleled my life at this very moment. I didn't know what was going to come of Ty and I. I knew that I wasn't going to keep letting this go on without commitment. Natalie's little sister Naphtali introduced me.

"Hi, as you've heard my name is Christina Sahara. Yes, it is like the desert. I tend to leave you thirsty when I'm done."

They laughed. The young college men gawked. Like always, I took a deep breath to calm my nerves and went for it but with so much emotion because this one was happening to me right now.

Tap Dance With The Serpent

I once tap danced with the serpent. He was fine and all that I thought I wanted in a man. One night he went into me and I was openly bare. I loved him and it didn't matter if he cared. I told myself lies that I was powerful and in tune with my sexuality. I was a woman you know and that should count for something. I never understood how I could love a spirit that didn't love me back. I thought I was empowered and it was just that. He laid up in me and looked dead in my soul. Me lying bare... naked and cold... I told myself we were equal and our needs were parallel. The lies I told myself were just comforts from hell. I laid there as his soul went deeper inside me... penetrating all that I thought I would be. Deep until my bones bled cold blood on his semen. I opened my wells and hell went up in it. I enjoyed the freedom of this mirage I had. I was free and nothing did ever mean that much to me. I called for him and he came in me and I tap danced all through that serpent's city. I knew his loveless "I love yous" were nothing to me but I accepted the charge because it was what "HE" said to me. Deep in my soul, he told the story of me before I even met him. I was hooked by his trance and I fell for him. Soon I will leave and never come back! He drew me in and I laid on my back. Opened bare to him, I moaned and screamed thinking somehow that would ease the pain. I put on my skin and jumped on his pole and rode his spirit with my eyes closed. Dry bones, they look and stare. Look at that wench lying bare. This time I'm leaving and never coming back! He sucked me right in and I crawled right back. Knees to hard ground, I liked his soul and his body too. Between his cheeks I kissed him and lay anew. I loved a soul that would never love me back. I was sucked in his trance and I was never leaving that. This time I'm leaving and never coming back! He forced my wells wide and drilled deeper in my garden. Lying bare I cried and moaned and screamed knowingly giving every piece of me. Yes, I am leaving and never coming back! He drove two fingers in my soul and laid me on my back. He looked to my spirit and tightened up the chains. Lying there, I was a poor, dirty maim. Deeper he went into my soul and grabbled every piece of me. Lifeless and soulless, I had to get up and run free. Surely I say, I am leaving and never coming back! He brushed up against me and I fell to my knees… sucking his soul out of him between his and these…. Then suddenly I return and lay bare on my back… his soul going deeper as my spirit cried. I moaned and moaned trying to wipe the pain from my eyes. Today I am leaving and never coming back! Just then I left and never looked back. Yes, I tap danced with the serpent and I remember it all so clear. Five years a slave to him… day in each and every year. I always dream of doing it again, but I thing of the loveless "I love yous" and the painful tears. I am free and whole again. Not another five years! I lied to myself a thousand times over. My needs are not equal and I'm better than his game. I tap danced with the serpent and at a time I lost my name. Yes, I think about the time we had and one could have never understood. I tap danced with a serpent before. I wish I would have stood. Stop telling myself these lies I cover to make myself feel true. When you tap dance with the serpent, the only thing you lose is you.

When that was over, I bowed and Naphtali hugged me so tight. She thanked me for coming and I thanked the class for having me and I left.

Ch. 13

There was so much to do in so little time. My phone had just reminded me that I had set a girls day out at the spa tomorrow and I had a short mini event to do early in the night. On my not so free time, I decided to get some other work done like calling the different real estate companies to see if I can take a look at the properties that my manager and others had told me about. All of them went straight to voicemail. How in the world was this going to help me? Out of pure torture, I called my mom.

"Hey mom, how are you?"

"I'm doing well. How about yourself? Have you found a place yet?"

"I'm okay. I haven't found a place yet, but I'm still looking."

"Why?"

"Ma'am?"

"I asked you how you were doing and you said "I'm okay". A mother can tell when something's wrong so you might as well tell me."

"Tyler and I got into a fight. No big deal."

"He bet not have put his hands on you"

"No mom, it wasn't like that."

"Then what was it?"

"I really don't want to talk about it."

"Listen here, I'm glad you both aren't seeing each other. Y'all been under each other like a baby to a nipple. Breathe girl! Take a break for a chance. Now I know what happens with these kinds of relationships but I've also realized that you have to learn for yourself. One day mom and pops won't be here when you and your siblings are going through the rough patches and it will be up to you all to figure this mess out."

"I know and eventually I will. For now, I just think he needs his space."

"You both do! You can't grow a living thing if you smother it."

Sometimes my mother talks in riddles but I understand her.

"I understand mama, but I just wish he would verbally come out and say how he feels already."

"A man will say it in his own right. Like your pops say, "A man knows within six months if you are the "one" for him." He may not say it but he's observing and watering the precious flower that he adores so much. You don't need to rush that man into telling you how he feels. You also don't need to wait like a sitting duck until he does."

"Then what am I suppose to do mama?"

"You're suppose to go and live your life. Keep travelling the world. If that man is meant for you then he will be there for you. In order to get the man, you have to be who you are looking for. Be that Proverbs 31 woman that I raised you to be. I know you are capable of being that. Lockdown the chocolate factory until further notice. Just live a little. Stop making a friend into the husband he's not. If he is then let God show you that. Do what you are called to do. If that man wants to be apart of your life, let him choose to. If you choose for him, I promise you, he will regret being with you for the rest of his life."

"I get what you are saying."

"I know there's a "but" coming. There is no "but". In life, you have to be what you are destined to be and let him be the same. There is no fifty-fifty in a relationship. I cannot give you half of me. It's all or nothing. I don't get why these young folks today are going around talking about "a relationship is fifty-fifty". A relationship is pouring out all of yourself to each other. That means always being transparent to one another. When you are married the two become one."

"I know that mama."

"The word says a man shall leave his father and cling to his wife. That means that whatever goes on in your marriage stays in your marriage. Half of these young folks telling every mistake that they and their partner make and wonder why when they are on good terms everyone hates them together. You can't tell your parents everything that goes on in your relationship and/or marriage. Let that stay between what God joined together."

I know my mama can talk. What started out as a checking in on her turned to see how she was doing turned into a two hour mini counseling session. My mother should have went into marriage counseling is what she should have done. She has great advice. Although that advice comes from her own trial and error but everyone needs a mom like mine. All my friends have adopted her anyway. They all call her mom and come to her for advice. Maybe she should start an advice column. That would save my ears from burning and my arms from going numb for holding the phone so long.

"Mom, it was nice talking to you. I have to go. I have a performance tonight and I have got to be there on time."

"I guess I'll have to talk to you later then huh?"

"I love you mama"

"Love you too, goodbye"

"Bye"

I went through my closet about three times trying to find something to wear to this event. Nothing seemed to be exactly how I wanted it. I just got frustrated and threw together some black leggings and a long sweater dress and some black pumps. My hair was natural so I just took it out of the pineapple (style that is basically a high ponytail for curly hair to preserve the curls longer), shook it till it looked how I wanted it to, locked up my house, turned the alarm on, and was down the road to some club close by my alma mater. I was happy to be going first this time around. I liked going first because I could get it over with and I didn't have to wait. I loved going last because the saying goes "You save the best for last". Am I right? I did my regular routine for getting rid of my nervous jitters and I walked on to the stage which was off to the side and I made sure I spoke up.

Departed Friendships

We were a triumvirate set of souls stuck together like Velcro. I intertwined and our bodies synchronized as if we all were one body menstruating at once. Mood swings and love things… deep feelings and cursing… burned tears and long years… a mirage was that we were inseparable and could not be shaken… dropped down like the Berlin wall… but it all changed… and we separated… disconnected… as if we never knew we existed… like we've never cried on each other… or fought for one another's safety… like distant souls we unfolded… torn apart like a wall of hands in red rover… walked on like the backs of slaves once over.. tossed away like a mother signing adoption papers… ripped apart like a child accustomed to a normal life… departed as if we were never on one page… this triumvirate group like the three musketeers, vanished… diminished like we weren't inseparable for years… oh distant souls… we walk away and say adieu… departed from me…I never knew you…

I was so glad that was over. I rushed to the bathroom real quick and went face first throwing up. The first thing that came to my mind was I better not be pregnant. I already knew what it was. I had a pill for nausea that I put under my tongue till it dissolved and I cleaned my face and walked out. I went to the bar and bought a sprite. I finished that and left. I went home. It was so great to be in my bed. It was even better to not have to share it with anyone. I didn't have to worry about any jungle sleepers. Those are the ones that sleep all over the place. I mean can I sleep in peace? I slept a total of six hours of sleep that night without being bothered about sex. I was thinking about what my mom said about celibacy. I really wanted to restart that journey but I only tend to last a year. Things always came up. Well Ty always came up. Then we were back in the same habit of coexisting. We were needing each other more than equally wanting each other. That is a big difference. We became a drug. Co-dependent on each other's sex. We became addicted. We were shooting each other up through our veins but simultaneously slowly killing each other off emotionally. We were drained. Mom was right a long time ago. I'd never tell her that.

Ch. 14

Finally it was the weekend. It was a day out with my girls. We get to finally catch up on life again. I packed some clothes for an overnight getaway at the Renaissance Birmingham Ross Bridge Golf & Spa. We weren't going golfing at all but the spa was all day for us. I carried my overnight bags to the car and locked up the house with the alarm. I headed down 65S then took interstate 459. Then I got off on Ross Bridge Pkwy and headed to the spa. As I was pulling into one of the parking spots closer to the door, I could see the girls with their luggage and ready to relax. We all shared the same suite. Everyone got dressed and headed downstairs for the facials first.

"Hey, where's Sara?"

"She couldn't make it this time" Britt said.

"You know there is always something going on. That man keeps her on a tight leash." Jennifer stated with that awful side-eye facial expression again.

"How do you you know? You don't know her life like that." Nat stated.

"She tells enough to not have to know her personally that well." Jennifer said.

Sometimes I just want to strangle that girl. Like everyone goes through things. Just because Sara seems like an open book doesn't mean everyone has to talk about her behind her back.

"Jennifer, I wouldn't talk if I were you." Britt stated.

"What you mean?"

"Hell your life is a walking open book. You don't have to say a damn thing for the rest of your life because we've seen every unprofessional sloppy sextape. Kim K wannabe!" Britt said.

"She getting paid isn't she" Jennifer said.

"That's her life though. You can't base yours off hers and think you're going to get the same treatment just because you're both Armenian." Britt stated.

"Shut up!" Jennifer yelled.

"Only because I'm right. The truth hurts bitch!"

"I got your ..."

I know I did not come up here to get away from drama just to be the referee for the main event.

"Y'all got to cut that out now. I did not invite you all up here to be acting like you're classless." I said.

"Act like you have some sense." Nat said.

"Don't start none, won't be none!" Britt said.

"I'm from Compton. We got all day." Jennifer said.

"I'm from Bed-Stuy. Space and opportunity!" Britt replied.

Lord, I did not come here for two street girls to act like they didn't get their degrees from elite universities.

"Cut it out! We came here to have fun and dammit we're going to have fun." I said.

I tell you it seems like the only ones sane is Natalie and I. Natalie is the oldest (29), myself (28 (29 this summer)), Brittani and Sara will be twenty-nine in August and you know it Jennifer is twenty-seven. Jennifer is the feistiest. I wish she was more civilized but that is not my problem. My mom says you should watch the company you keep. She never liked Jennifer either but back in the day Jennifer was funny and spontaneous. She would have you in the craziest situations as well. After everyone had calmed down and was lined up for the massages, we started getting into our usual girl chat. I made them promise to keep Sara's name out of it. We're grown and things don't need to be said behind someone else's back. If you have a problem by now then you should address it woman to woman. We are too old for this petty betty shit.

"Guys, have anyone of you tried the "V- steam"?" I asked.

"What is that?" Natalie and Britt asked.

"It's where you sit your naked butt on this toilet thing and it is steaming hot and it cleanses you. It suppose to be like a steam douche." Jennifer answered.

"Does it hurt?" Natalie asked.

"Not really" Jennifer replied.

"I read that it isn't good for you." I said.

"You got to live a little. Try it just once then decide for yourself. If you hate it then you never have to worry about it again."

"Yeah, but I'm not going through that." I said.

After we had finished doing the facials, we decided to get a deep tissue massage.

Ch. 15

Getting up on that skinny table was a pain. I asked the attendant to find me a step stool. I am too short for this mess. The girls were making jokes about my height but I brushed it off. When she finally came back with the steel, black step stool. I stood on top of it and pushed myself onto the table. Heads laying against the soft cushioned head rest. The masseuse began to run oils that smelled like sweet almond oil and lavender. It felt so good to get every ache massaged out. I specifically needed my legs massaged because I have been going so much that I haven't had time to relax. Sometimes my legs would tingle then go numb. Other times they would just ache. I don't know if it was from the squatting exercises or being on the go so much and not letting my body rest a while. No one even spoke a word during the massage segment. We were pretty much calmed down and half sleep or nodding off. It was the quietest that I have seen us collectively as a whole. I kind of like it. Maybe, I liked it a little too much. The girl massaging me switched for a guy. I couldn't see his face but his cologne smelled like Polo Blue. It was very enticing. He started rubbing my glutes in a circular motion. Then his hands went up and down my inner thigh like it was waiting for the green light to go a little further. That was not what they could do by law. Now I've heard of places that give the happy endings. I am very leary about living a little when I don't know where the hell their hands been. They could have gotten herpes from those other happy endings and trying to massage them into me. Just nasty I tell you. You just don't know where these people's hands have been. I have been here multiple times in several occasions. I get the same person so I know plus I keep tabs on those who touch me. Professionally, your place of work should be clean, sanitized, and you should have double gloved if you have an open sore with a bandaid on that sore. I'm ruthless when you don't come correct and try to mess up my health. Like these nail salons that don't change water at the foot stations or don't clean their utensils. I bring my own utensils and I make them and watch them clean that water before I stick my feet in them. If there's an infection in my body, it was caused by germs in the air or genetics but it won't be caused by carelessness. Not on my watch! The final thing we did for the evening was get our nails did before dinner. We were all at different stations getting French manicures with different color tips. I preferred the blue tips but regular manicure. The other girls liked those pointy nails. They looked ugly to me but it was just not my preference. After all day of getting pampered, we decided to head back to our rooms, wash up and change, and get dinner. We all ordered the wine and I ordered the cheapest meal on the menu. I'm the type of woman that won't spend a whole lot of money on a meal when I don't know where the chef's hands been. Yeah, call me crazy but the exquisite meals need to be done by someone I trust. As much as I've been here, I still don't trust people. We all waited till the food was served. We blessed the food and began to talk about the most random things from hair to fashion to guys to sex.

"Oh my gosh, I was watching the tennis match up. You all know Serena is my girl. They were saying that she was taking performance drugs. I know my girl don't take those. They're just saying that because they can't beat her." Britt started out.

"You know, the people that are the main ones to call you out on something is trying to tell you that they are really the culprits." I said.

"You're right." Jennifer replied.

"I just don't understand how you can downsize a person's talent and/or gift because you cannot win against them. Sometimes I think race does come into play. They've called her everything and she's still successful." Natalie said.

"She always will be. They can never beat someone of her caliber and poise because it all starts from within." I said.

"They're looking real ugly if you ask me. Jennifer replied.

"What about that kid who got shot up north?" Britt asked.

I know this was going to be a heated, touchy conversation. When you begin to talk about race in public, the masquerade masks begin to come off. Whatever was hidden before is now transparent on the surface.

"That was a sad story. I followed the whole thing. For them to lie knowing that they watched that child die and didn't even call for an ambulance was messed up." I said.

"You can say it. They were some fucked up pieces of shits. How can you watch someone else's child die and do nothing? I know for a fact they wouldn't be doing that if it was their own child." Jennifer said in anger.

"When I seen that mother on television talking about her pain, I broke. I cried so hard for her. Her child won't be able to go to high school, experience prom, go to college or none of the other life successes." Natalie said.

"I cried as well. I thought to myself what if that was my child." Britt said.

I don't know what it was about dinner, but our most intense conversations always tend to start at dinner.

Britt kept talking. "I'm very hard on my sons and I would be devastated if something were to happen to them. They're going to their father's this summer and I would like to think they would be safe when they are out with their friends or anyone else for that matter. I don't want to get the call in the middle of the night that says my son has been murdered. I just don't know what I would do but I wouldn't be able to handle that." Britt said.

"Even though I don't have kids yet, I sometimes feel scared to raise them in a society like this. A society where we all have to basically stalk our children with video cameras and audio just to make sure they are safe. Make sure that they are with us at all times." I said.

"I just don't understand why when I talk to people of other races about what we go through, it seems like a myth. Nothing is a myth. Until they have walked a mile in my shoes then they basically have nothing to say to me about racism and racial profiling." Britt said.

What had started out as a rowdy but then peaceful day was turning into an emotional time over dinner. Once we had all paid for our separate meals, we went back upstairs. We all hung out in the living room area. Everyone had changed into something comfortable except Jennifer. Jennifer loved to wear her birthday suit. That's why we never really invite her over for overnight girls day. I was wearing red plaid pajamas with my black hanes socks. Natalie was always the camisole (teal) and some Mickey mouse boyshorts. Brittani had on the full out onesie with the zipper low enough that if she bent over her boobs would pop out. Everyone knew that there was nothing under that onesie. We basically had two girls in real pajamas, one without, and one who was half zipped without. I mean Jennifer had this phase where she thought she was into girls but she wasn't all in. She was literally just scratching the surface. Back in college, Jennifer had a crush on Brittani. One drunk night at our sleepovers they became an item and they never knew it. I was still up at the time and still to this day never bothered to tell them. Yes, Jennifer had had her hands anywhere she could get as far as Brittani was concerned. That night, Britt, Jennifer, and I were all drunk. Somehow Britt and Jennifer started arguing about something. I really can't remember. Then Jennifer, as naked as she can be, started fighting Britt. She had unzipped that onesie and had ripped it off of her. Now Jennifer and Britt are both naked fighting. I'm still zoned out. I'm watching them roll on top of each other back and forth. All of a sudden it happened. Jennifer started kissing Britt in the mouth. Tongues wrapped around the other. Still fighting, she pushed Britt to the floor and pinned her down. Next thing I knew she was softly licking Britt's pussy until it was wet. Britt started moaning and with every lick Jennifer had, Britt squirmed. I was looking like what the hell was I watching. Nope, never joined in. I wasn't into that kind thing. I don't think Britt was either. Once Britt had came in Jennifer's mouth, they both passed out. I kept it to myself because I know Britt hates that girl with a passion. To know that one day that they were more intimate than they thought would drive her crazy.

Ch. 16

Now we didn't talk much after that long day. We all walked to our separate rooms and fell asleep. The next day we had all showered and packed up. We said our good-byes to each other and departed the resort. Next time we would have to make it somewhere away from home. I drove back home off of I-65 and traffic was good on this Sunday morning. I was battling so much in my mind that I didn't know whether to go to church or stay at home and get ready for the event later tonight. My weeks started to get hectic. Daniel had started booking me everywhere. Some days I would fly to California then to New York. Other days I'd drive to Miami then Tallahassee. I never knew where I would end up or when I would slow down. I had this gut feeling that life wouldn't slow down for me any sooner. I had stated a long time ago that I wanted my life to pick up. I wanted to be booked, overbooked, and blessed. With all of that comes the tests as well. Well this time I was headed to the Bohemia Room in Miami. We drove those looked like eleven hours to the lower part of Florida. You know my thing is once the car gets out of the city then I have my music blasting in my beats headphones knocked out cold. I'm a sleep rider. I don't stay awake in cars. Once I'm in, I doze off. We arrived in Miami around seven or eight at night. I found the W where we could check-in. I freshened up and got back into the rented Lexus and headed to the club to perform. I was opening and closing tonight. I started with "Wake Up" because it's something we all need to hear. The DJ was playing some old school R. Kelly. I was grinding in my chair. I told Daniel to go buy me a long island iced tea. I don't go to the bars. I let him get it because I know that if I get it for myself someone will always try something stupid. I'm already nervous and I don't need to be drugged either. When the host called me to the stage, I was very ancy. There were so many people in the room. Too many girls under dressed. Their leave out didn't match the weave that they had. Some girls were wearing see through liquid dresses and right when they went to dance, their pussies were all out for the men to see. The men were dressed like they were either in the nineties or just left wall street. There were no in between. As usual, I closed my eyes to begin with and began to speak.

Wake Up!

Wake up! This world is a cannon dismembered in a war. A gun forced in lock at battle. Our tongues are cut out like we have no first amendment right r refuse to use it. Being used and manipulated by those who shove their right to use it first. I have the right to talk. Just like you have the right to defend the weak or get lost… no identity amongst the crowd… I am no shadow to the sins of the earth and I have a voice to speak. I will not be sussurant with my voice because you're offended by the truth. Grow some balls! Feel some pain and wake up because the war is going on with or without you. I am not sussurant nor am I the lie you tell to pacify yourself. Wake up! Say it… be true to your right… there are too many things in disarray so you have no option left… rise up and fight!

After that was done, I went back to my table and watched the others perform. There was this one poet they called P2 who was nothing but smooth. He was suave and articulate. He talked about his fatherhood experience. He was the sexiest of the poets. If I wasn't trying to practice celibacy then I would have tried to send off some kind of body language that I wanted him. I just enjoyed the crowd. I watched one couple fuss about how the man was staring at the other girls in those liquid dresses. Dresses so tight you could surely rip them apart and they would stand in their birthday suits. One old guy was giving me this look in this played out jheri curl and gold teeth. His teeth looked like he abandoned them. I just hoped he never walked my way. Thank God he didn't! I sure got a sniff of him when I went to use the bathroom. I'd give any girl this advice, "Squat always". Club bathrooms are the worse when you have to do any number. You better hope you don't have to take a dump because you'd be praying that your butt don't catch staph from sitting on that toilet. The other artists had finished their sets and it was time for me to close out. I chose "I Am Africa" because we are all apart of Africa even if we weren't born there. Our roots still tell the story and our DNA is the proof to defend it. I walked on stage proud this time to speak. I didn't hold anything back.

I Am Africa

I was the totem of the world sitting high. I was the first connection to heaven until my people betrayed me... Sold my precious gems for irreplaceable objects... took my DNA like spilled blood on a pavement... walked over by simplistic idiots not repaying the whipped backs of pain I've been through... burying tears in my roots for all the years they never came back to see me... they never came home to meet me... I was first made for kings and queens... now my people seem to mirror the western sins of the one who raped me... took my soul and ripped my love... my DNA taken from me... deceived by my own like a native genocide... I hid behind my knowledge like Eve in my garden... I was the totem of the earth... fallen off... cried out... mourned no more... give me back my people and put me on the throne... I was the totem of the earth ... I am Africa!

Ch. 17

I was on a roll and from there I had to stay in Miami for another night because I had another event at Club Luck off of 19th St. We headed back to the hotel after it closed and I crashed. I know people have asked me if something was going on between Daniel and I but we are strictly business. Daniel is a sweet man but that ex of his is enough to stay away. Sometimes I would babysit Jr. occasionally. It's probably been roughly five times. The twins are private men. Now David has liked me since before I could remember. I don't know why we never tried to make something more from our friendship. I know his eyes light up when we're trying to do business. We've hung out many of times just the two of us but it was just between friends. The next morning I had room service ordered for breakfast and I just relaxed all day in my room knowing that I was free until tonight. Everyone knows what I basically did all day. I slept. Daniel was on the phone making some business calls. I don't actually think that he has ever just relaxed. Daniel lived for Polo shirts, Dickies, and Sperries. He dressed like a prep boy. His brother was the business suit guy. They were almost total opposites. I've always wondered if identical male twins have the "twin thing" like identical female twins. I wouldn't know. They say they don't have it but you can see the angst in their expressions when they are away from each other for a long period of time. I think that is why I hired them as a package deal. You just know when your siblings need one another. They are one that remains very close. I mean two grown men ... Well it's just hard to explain ... You just have to see them in person together. Well the night came and it was time to perform for my last night in Miami. I was so ready to get this over with and head to my king size bed, 1200 count Egyptian cotton threaded sheets, and my jacuzzi tub in the master bedroom at home. I got in the car and fell asleep as usual. Daniel woke me up when we got to the club. It was the Addicted Version tonight. I was suppose to perform opposite side the strippers for a ladies night in. This is when I definitely had to close my eyes to keep from getting distracted from what I was going to say. Their oiled up bodies were not helping my case any. I looked up to the ceiling and said "Lord, don't let me stray tonight." I decided not to start with the deep breath and just go for it.

Addicted Ecstasy

Come in… drop it all and sit… surrender to the taste of my love as it drops like rain on your tongue… come closer into the realm of my being… suit and tie you stand there as I embrace your body and trace the sweat of your face slowly dripping your articles… painting my kisses down your back… I glow and blow below… let my hands lather sweet lavender oils on your forever enticing body enriched with love for the least of these… let my love connect to your spirit till you awaken when you hear it… hear the falsetto like screams crescendoing in our air. Let me please the midway of your hearts window… let my body thrust against yours …stroking you till your eyes tell me you can't handle it… till your lips whisper enough… let me satisfy your senses … be your fiend… your addiction… come closer and let me be your maverick… blow your mind… making love in a land of none… let me explore the depths of your imagination… and hold tightly as I send you into deep ecstasy… addicted to your crevices… I am your drug and you are my addict… taking over your body like fire from a volcano, we breathe… addicting… and seducing… let me show you where you stand… addicted and bare like my inner hand… Now feel me… Aaah

That was finished. I bowed. I shook the hands of the host and thanked her for inviting me. The strippers wanted a hug but I gave them a handshake and walked away. After we got back in the car, I was hyped for a long time. I stayed woke for most of the ride back. My eyes got real heavy real quickly and I fell asleep. After that long ride back home, all I wanted was to see my bed. I turned the alarm off and unlocked the door. I went inside and waved at Daniel so he could tell the driver to leave. I walked in and to my surprise, here was Tyler standing in my doorway.

"What are you doing here?"

"I missed you."

"That's not what I asked."

"I wanted to see you."

"Look, I've had a long couple of days and all I waant to do is go upstairs, soothe myself in my tub with some jazz playing, then take my ass to bed."

"Can I hold you for a minute?"

Ty tried to lean in to hug me but I stepped back.

"I can't do this right now. I'm tired."

"Just hear me out."

"I really am not going to do this right now. You need to leave."

"Tina, please"

"No! Leave Ty!"

"Please, just hear me out. I just need ten minutes of your time."

He started to grab me. I pulled away and headed to my room. He grabbed my luggage and followed.

"You need to leave Ty. I can't --"

Ty started kissing me on my neck. He tried to use every touch down my body to get me to listen. I quickly pulled away from that.

"Please!"

You can tell he was getting frustrated. His eyes started tearing up. I started unpacking my clothes and undressing. It was no point in getting him to leave so I just ignored him. I could have pushed him out the door but there was still something that was unresolved. Mom was right again. That soul tie was wrapped around us so tight that we felt we needed each other rather than wanting to love each other. I took off my socks and went into the bathroom and turned on the water to the jacuzzi. I made sure that it was hot but not too hot to burn me. It had to be just right to soothe my muscles. After I poured the lavender bubble bath soap in the water, I waited until it filled up a little over half way and then I eased down in the tub. I grabbed the remote and turned on the jazz station. I leaned back, closed my eyes, and soaked my aching body. I heard pants unzip. Ty was a softie. He was hard for everyone else but around me he was putty. I heard the water splash when he got in. He just eased open my legs and sat between them. His back facing me he laid his head back on my chest. He closed his eyes and we both just sat there in the jacuzzi in perfect silence. We almost fell asleep in there. I broke the ice first.

"You have five minutes"

"Huh!"

"Whatever you were going to say, I'm giving you five minutes to say it."

"I messed up babe. I apologize for what I said before. I know you do care. I care about you too."

"You sure as hell don't act like it."

"I was just frustrated with work and I know that I shouldn't have taken it out on you. For that I am truly sorry."

"I forgive you now but there won't be a next time. We talk out our problems not go off on each other."

He stood up and eased out of the tub. He helped me out of the tub and I grabbed a towel to dry off. I went to my dresser to find my pajamas and I put them on. I just felt like wearing a white cami and some shorts tonight. I pulled back the covers and eased in bed after I pulled my curls back and covered my hair with my satin bonnet and made sure I was double secured with the satin pillowcase. Ty actually thought he was going to get laid after that apology but I turned the other way and went to sleep.

Ch. 18

I woke up with a reminder that tonight was the 90s themed party at FAMU tonight. Home of the rattlers. It was about to bring me into my childhood real quick. There was an open mic night going on, a 90s gear contest, and an old fashioned Uncle Luke dance off for the girls. There was just so much to do. I checked online for all of the commercial properties. I checked out how big the parking was because I hate to be in a place where the parking sucked. I was about to call mom when she called me first.

"Hey mom, I was just about to call you. How are y'all down there?

"Everything is fine. I was calling to see if you had heard from Sara."

"No ma'am. She was suppose to go to the spa with us this past weekend but she never showed. I thought she was on call lately."

"That was the weekend before. She has been acting mighty strange lately. I just can't put my finger on it."

"If something's going on I know you will find out before the next day."

My mother was always one to call the hotline queen. That's what we called her friends. They knew everything from the city. My pops knew every cop in the state. If anything criminal went down, he knew first hand. My pops was the man. He had his own security business. He was very tough on us even though we weren't his kids. He was the only father I knew since I can remember. Telling that story would be a whole other story.

"I'll call Lena and see what's going on."

"How are you really mom?"

"I'm fine. I won't let this life control me. My circumstance won't break me either."

My mother was headstrong. I admired her for her courage. I knew she had it hard growing up but to me she will always be the one I'd always look up to.

"How's life since I see you rarely pick up your phone?"

"Life is good. It seems to be picking up speed as well."

"You say that as if it is a bad thing."

"I want my life to pick up and be booked but I also want to be balanced and actually enjoy living it."

"You have to make sure you keep that in mind. This life you're going after will catapult you into a world so much different than your own. You have to stay grounded to your beliefs, morals, and standards in order to make it past the tempting parts."

"I know that. I'm just ready to see what life is."

"Don't rush things ever. You never know what is on the other side of the fast life. Yes, you might have the financial freedom but with everything there is a price. How much are you willing to sacrifice? How far are you willing to go to get it?"

"I'm not going to get into any of that stuff. I just want to live my life how it is but a little more cushioned."

"Tina, life happens. There are things in life that are out of our control. Not everything is a temptation to us. Somethings are merely pain that we cannot control."

I didn't say anything. I knew how she was talking that she wasn't telling me something. With mothers, you might never know what they really know until it happens or you happen to stumble upon it. Well I knew after that long silence that I might as well end the conversation.

"Mom, I have to go get some rest. It's two in the afternoon and I have got to be ready to be on the road to head to Florida when the twins get here."

I don't know why I keep saying "the twins" as if they didn't have their own separate identities. I guess I was so used to it by now that it became second nature.

"Oh, how are my boys?"

"They're fine mama but I really have to go now"

"Well I will talk to you later then. I love you."

"I love you too mama."

I hung up. Then I fell asleep on the couch. Ty was staying at his place since I was going out of town. I couldn't be more relieved. I'm starting to love him. Who am I kidding? I've loved that man since college. When I woke up, it was already time to go and Daniel was banging on my front door as if he thought I had gotten shot.

"I'm coming! Stop banging on my door before I make you pay for a new one."

"We're running late."

"That doesn't mean you have to kick the door down just to get me to open."

"Let's go. We have a long drive"

"Don't you think I know that?"

I don't know what was up with Daniel but he was working my last nerve." Sometimes I wonder how they are identical, raised in the same house, but he winds up a little less mature than David. We headed out on the road to Tallahassee, Florida. When we started seeing some palm trees then we knew we had hit the Florida line. We got there about five minutes late. That stigma that black people were always late. That would be one to keep for most of us. Man there were some fine men in the room. Some were my age and some looked like they were still wet behind the ears or still had a mouth that smelled like breastmilk. These were some babies if I've never seen any. I was just ready to get this over with so I could party. About ten minutes after we had settled in on campus, the event people finally started to start this thing. You seen some girls dressed like hoochie mamas. They were ready to get lit but not in a good way. I started it off with my memories of the 90s.

90's Kid

It's not the same… standing here as the world changed… I remember when parents knew their kids friends name… when all I needed to worry about was chores… when the only thing they could take from me was video games… mortal kombat and sonic… blowing on cartridges after we ripped it out of the system because the computer was cheating… staying all night at the table till we finished everything on our plates… and talking back would get you knocked into the next day… when the only thing you snuck to watch was HBO on s broken channel blurred out by censorships… where watching sex scenes through warm hands on your face was the regular… where imaginations soared and children explored the world around them… where power rangers was the group everyone had to act out on the playground… where three ninjas kickback, surf ninjas, and karate kid made everyone want to learn martial arts… where teenage mutant ninja turtles was the show on Saturday mornings and watching recess was the "before school" ritual… where trading Pokèmon cards and Dragon ball Z was the boys card game to beat… Where did all of it go? … Sucked up by Ghostbusters in an open black hole… I wish I could go back to my childhood again… because lost dreams and hurt things, bills and sufferings ain't what I meant when I rushed getting older…. I just wanted to do as adults did but still remain me, young… that scrawny, kick butt, imaginative kid… I just wanted to grow up but still be a 90s kid…

I took a bow and then I grabbed Daniel's hand and we hit the dance floor. They had a playlist of songs like "Capt. D Comin'", Ride That Train", Juvenile's "Back That Ass Up", and Sisqo's "Thong Song" and a host of others. I mean every girl sweated out their perms. It looked like sex on the dance floor. There was so much to do. Then they took it old school 90s with Kid N Play's "Roll With Kid and Play". The older crew started singing along and the guys were doing the house party dance. Then here came the songs the girls song to "TLC" "No Scrubs", "KP & Envy" "Swing My Way" and countless others. I had so much fun bringing back my childhood that I really didn't want to leave. We stayed to see the winners of the different contests. This six foot two, tall, slim brotha with the high top fade won the contest for the 90s gear. He was dressed like Kid from Kid N Play hands down. Man they played "Big Booty Hoes" and these girls were bumping and grinding. This big butt girl with the little black dress and nails so long they could wrap around the steering wheel won the contest for the dancing. Hell, she might as well. She had hit every guy with her butt by just walking. She dropped a split right down the center of one of the judges so they had to give it to her. They were still playing music when we left. They started the 90s slow jams mix. I fell asleep in the car.

Ch. 19

We had to drive all the way to Troy University in Troy, Al to perform "The Father's Lift" for a program that was geared toward kids with incarcerated parents. The drive was quite long so I finally was knocked out. I started dreaming of my own paternal father. I dreamed of how everything would have been had his life wouldn't have taken a turn for the worst. We were just sitting in the park talking. I could remember asking him if he loved me and looked down on me and said always. I barely have memories of my paternal father. I don't know if we'll have that freedom to make more than what was already embedded in my head. I couldn't think of that part. I had to think on the now. If I can help the now then I can change my future. I needed so bad to change how I saw my future. We got to Troy about seven in the morning. At this point all I wanted to do was say what I had to say and move on. I didn't want to go deep in my feelings. I just wanted to say what I came here to say and leave. I got there and my voice started feeling scratchy. This will not happen to me today and just my luck no one carried honey, cough drops, cough syrup, or allergy pills. I knew that I was running myself thin but I had to keep pushing myself in order to get to where I needed to be. I hit the stage and I performed. It wasn't with a whole lot of passion because I was completely drained. I still pushed myself anyway. Sometimes you just have to push through it all. I just opened my mouth and out came the words.

The Father's Lift

My father once lifted me above his head… stared me deep in my eyes and said I love you with his. Love, a bond so tied it, it was more than just bliss. I was from his love and I became his heart. Growing and growing, you'd think we'd never grow apart. Memories upon memories of running into his arms lifting me up so the world could do no harm. Wiping away tears to take away my pain, he loved me that much. He wanted that moment to stay the same. Falling asleep in his arms as he cradled me like a cub… Sleeping in protection was the moment he poured out his love. Sweet minutes of these as I rested upon his chest… Let me know a father's love was the very best… there would be no man greater than this who would lift me for protection like the world wouldn't be missed. Sweet giggles and soft kisses upon my cheek … none other than the father who saw his mirror image in me… vaguely I recall other times when he ran… but this day when he lifted me, a fortress in his hands.

Ch. 20

When that was over, we got in the car and headed back home. I though that I would be able to rest and catch up on much needed sleep. That never worked. The time I pulled up to my house and said goodbye to Daniel, my phone rang. It was Sara.

"Hey Sara, how are you?

"I need you to come to St. Vincent"

"Why? What's wrong Sara? Did he hurt you again?

"I just need you to hurry!"

Sara sounded frantic. She seemed distressed. I didn't know what had happened to her but I knew that I had to find out as soon as possible.

"Where are you?"

"I'm at St. Vincent East."

I knew proper protocol was to keep abuse victims out of the system. It protects their privacy. I didn't know if I could come see her.

"I'm on my way."

We hung up the phone and every fear that I ever had flashed across my mind. I didn't know how far he had taken it. I didn't know how bad it was. I've been there through it all. I still don't see why she married him. If a man is abusive before the marriage then why marry him in the first place? People tell me that you don't know until you get into this situation. I've seen too many of these same situations to know when to exit. Sara stayed in Ensley so I don't know how she got to my side of town. I figured she thought he wouldn't be able to find her. Sara was the bread winner in her family. Although her parents died in such a tragic death, Sara had a trust fund. She could have did way much better with her life. I'm not one to judge because my life after I left home wasn't speckle free either. I met her at St. Vincent and it was bad. Sara had a black eye, two broken ribs, a busted lip, a broken tooth, and a gash on the side of her head. Her vitals were stable at the time. Sara has always had trouble with her blood pressure. It was either too high or too low. There was no in between.

"Hey sunshine, I'm here"

Sara started tearing up as she turned her head to look at me. I could see the pain in her eyes. Her tears were warm as I wiped them with my thumb.

"I'm glad you came."

"You know I couldn't let you stay here by yourself."

Trying to fight the tears from falling I said, "I love you. I need you to know that and I would do anything for you. We're sisters. We may not be blood but we're sisters."

"Sisters for life"

"Sisters for life"

"How did this happen?"

"It's nothing. I just fell and got a few cuts and scrapes."

I know she didn't think I was stupid.

"Cuts and scrapes? Cuts and scrapes is not a black eye and broken ribs. Cuts and scrapes is not a gash on your head. What the hell happened? Did Thomas do this?"

"Like I told you, I fell. It's nothing."

"Staying with a man that does this is not nothing."

"He's still my husband."

"He's a coward who is abusing you and is going to keep abusing you till you are no longer here. Do you want that?"

I was so mad at her.

"Stop yelling at me!"

I couldn't hold the tears back anymore.

"I just want you to know that you are beautiful. You are smart and strong. You don't need a man that is putting his hands on you."

"I know that."

"Then why are you still with him?"

"I don't know!"

"Wake up Sara! Do you want to keep living like this? Do you want to wake up enslaved like this? This man has done nothing for you."

"He's still my husband."

After that I knew there was no getting through to her. Nothing I said was going to make her walk away and understand her importance of living free. I stayed with her overnight. I'd occassionally watch her sleep. That night one of the techs came in to check her routine vitals. I guess he liked me. That was the vibe I was getting. He was an average four at best. One catch to it all he was married and still trying to pursue me.

"Hey Sara, I'm O'sina and I'm here to check your vitals."

He began to wrap the blood pressure cuff around her arm and turned the monitor on. Then he put the thermometer with the throw away clips in her mouth. All the while, he was staring at me. I looked at him from above my computer. He smiled. He motioned for me to come to him. I ignored him. He left. Later that night I was going to get some more towels so I could wash up and do my hair while I was at it. Kill two birds with one stone by using someone else's utilities. I tiptoed out of the room to the nurses station to get some towels and a blanket for this hideous couch that I was laying on. Low and behold, O'sina was there to retrieve what I had asked for. I had this sign that he wanted more than what his job intailed. Every time Sara hit the call light for pain medicine, assistance to the bathroom, juice, you name it, he answered. It's like he was stalking this room. Like he had to be in this room at all times. That night, I had layed down and was trying to go to sleep while Sara was resting. This fool came in to check her vitals again and while he waited, he decided he wanted to check me too. He ducked down in that cold, dark room and started groping my butt. Then he put his hand down my shirt and started sucking my nipples like he was malnourished for breastmilk. I was in shock at what was happening to me. My mouth wanted to say stop and scream for help. When I opened my mouth, my voice failed me. Nothing came out. I was laying on that pleather couch while this man just felt me up. My shorts were very loose on me. They were easy access to my yoni. I mean what the hell was happening here? My best friend had just been abused and is laying up in a hospital bed and here I am on this couch that I'm stuck to and getting assaulted by a man I didn't even know. He eased his hands between my legs and started shoving them up her. Her secret temple was being invaded by some man's nasty ass hands and my voice failed me. I tried pushing him away from me but he was stronger. He had more willpower. I couldn't break free. I couldn't breathe. All I could do was just lay there and let my body deceive me. It was overflowing with wetness for a guy I had never met before him. I was not enjoying this invasion of my privacy. The more I tried to push the words out, the more nothing would come out. I felt ashamed in myself for doing nothing. After thirty minutes of him hiding in the room assaulting me, he left and went to another room. When he left I exhaled and I cried silently. How could I let this guy get this close to me? How did this happen? What the hell? I cried myself to sleep that night. The next morning I woke up. I was too ashamed and embarrassed to tell anyone about what happened so I kept quiet. He should have lost his job but I never said a word. The doctors came by and checked her body to see how the stitches were going. They gave her some Norco for the pain. The discharge process took the longest time. I was so ready to go at that point.

Ch. 21

She didn't want breakfast but I made her eat it so we could get out of here. It was about three in the afternoon before they discharged her. The room smelled like mothballs and bengay anyway.

"I'm glad you get to get out of this place."

"I know."

"I'll bring the car around so we can go."

"That will be fine. You go ahead and go home. My ride is coming."

"I'm not leaving you here."

"I'll be fine. Just go home and get a real nice rest."

"Why are you trying to get rid of me so fast? Is he coming up here? I know you are not going home with him?"

"I have to! My kids are there and I don't want to split up my family. I don't want to argue with you or lose you either."

"You don't have to do this. I have room at my place that we can all go to. You won't ever have to worry about him."

"Like I said yesterday, I'm not splitting up my family. He is still my husband."

When Sara is adamant about something, she gets pigheaded sometimes. I don't want this to be the last time I see my friend. There's just too many things going on right now. I mean I wish I could tell her about what happened last night but I'm too worried about her. Thomas walked into the room with some roses and a teddy bear that he had to have found in someone's trash can. This bear was missing an eye and the cotton was visible through one of the feet. He smelled of Hennessey and vodka. His hair was unkempt but he was nicely dressed. He had a body odor of rotten eggs. I knew it wasn't just me that smelled it because the nurses were holding their breath walking pass him to get to her.

"What are you doing here?" I asked.

"This is my wife. I should be asking you this same thing." He said.

"This is my friend and I know what you did to her." I said.

"I didn't do a thing." He said calmly. It was like he was hiding something.

"You put her here!" I yeled.

"Like I said, this is my wife and you can leave. There's the door. Get the hell out!" Thomas said.

"I'm leaving but only because I do not want to start a scene. Sara I'll call you later." I said.

"Don't bother! She won't be contacting you again anyway." Thomas said.

I stormed out that room. I caught the elevator and headed to my car which was parked on the third level of the parking deck. I couldn't get to my car fast enough. When I got in there, I locked my door and banged my hands against the steering wheel. I screamed. I cried. I screamed through my teeth. I cranked up the car, paid my fee, and drove home. It didn't take me long to get there either. I don't know how fast I was going and I didn't care if the cops had stopped me either. They never showed. I pulled up in my driveway, opened the garage door and drove in. The door closed behind me. I unlocked my house, turned off the alarm, and went in. I needed someone to talk to. I didn't want to call my mom just yet so I called Brittani.

"Hey Tina, how are you?"

"I'm good."

"You've been crying?"

"No"

I know I'm not suppose to lie. I really didn't want to talk about what happened in it's entirety right now. I didn't know who else to talk to that wouldn't lecture me.

"Yes you have. What's going on? You can't hide from me. I know you."

"I stayed with Sara last night."

"You did what?! You actually stayed in the house with that bastard of a husband?"

"No, he put her in the hospital."

"Again?"

"Yeah"

"When is she going to leave that man?"

"Honestly, I don't know."

"Which hospital? I'm on my way."

"Don't bother. She was discharged today."

"Where did she go? Is she at your house?"

"Take a wild guess."

"She went back to him after all that?"

"Unfortunately"

"Why didn't you stop her?"

"And do what exactly? Aye, you can't go with him because you're going to get yourself killed."

"Something!"

I wondered if this was the right time to tell someone what had happened to me last night. Everyone has been so focused on Sara that they wouldn't care anyway. I am drained.

"Well she's with him now and there is nothing you or I can do about that."

"You should have called the police."

"Say what? With what evidence? You can't call the cops on a man when all she is going to do is bail him out anyway."

"Enough of this. It is making me mad. How was your weekend at FAMU?" She asked

"It was great, I should have stayed there longer." I replied.

I mumbled, "Maybe I wouldn't have to deal with this."

"Say something?"

"Nope"

I really wanted to tell her what had happened to me but I just couldn't. I guess I would have to deal with this on my own. I don't even know how to do that.

She kept on talking about hair expos, politics, her nasty custody battle, and how the kids were going to spend time with their dad for spring break which was in April. Moments later we finished talking and I hung up. I unpacked, did two loads of laundry, and fell asleep. I knew the next couple of months that I was going to be slam booked.

Ch. 22

I decided to throw myself into my craft. I woke up and started packing. I had two nights at the Soul Wired Café in Jackson, Mississippi. Daniel and David were in the black Cadillac escalade this time. I put my bags in the trunk and got in. We headed out to the state with the crooked letters. I really wanted to tell the twins about what happened to me the other night but I decided that it was a battle only I could fight. I'd have to deal with this the best that I knew how. When we got there, I guess the bar was to the back of the stage. More like the back of the room. The place was packed and dimly lit. Everyone was doing the snap thing. I never really got into snapping when an artist had a great piece. I just clapped like a mama would do on their child's first accomplishment. Clapped like I was saying "That's my baby". Clapped like I had won an award that was a long time coming. Clapped like I was Will Smith in the "Pursuit of Happiness". The smoke in that room was very thick. I didn't know how many cigarettes collectively people were smoking but it was making me lightheaded. I took a seat near the wall with the least amount of people around. People that I could see were not smoking. I opened the night up with "Reach For Heaven". All of these were short pieces so I was glad for it.

Reach For Heaven

I tried to reach for heaven, but I got a piece of you. The one in my midst, you stand filled with gratitude. I tried to reach for heaven to seek the glorious light, but he showed me your presence in your helping hand every day and night. I tried to reach for heaven to get a connection, direction to which I should run to, but he said run to the arms that love you. That birthed you… that made a way on this earth for you… I tried to reach for heaven to seek the whereabouts of my place, but he sent me down to turn a frown upside down and presented me to your face. I tried to reach for heaven, but the light shown through the gates. Because the one who sent me down here told me I'd put a smile on your face. Yeah, I tried to reach for heaven and I wanted earth no more. When I tried to reach for heaven, from your heart you poured out love more and more.

Then the crowed snapped their fingers and I bowed. The music played songs of Babyface, Kem, and R. Kelly. It was mellow. There were no wild, raunchy dancing. I waited for the other talent to finish just to close the night. One girl had long, thick, curls and she sung "I Can't Wait To Hate You" by The Dream very nicely. Some did the poetry and art. Others did some rapping and got the crowd to their feet. I was finally ready to end this night because I had another night here anyway. I dedicated this piece to my grandmother and took it away.

Backbone

I'm half of her and half of you. The backbone of your family has been gone… died on… it's chaotic… no one speaks… no one weeps… as if they never loved me… we never had a connection… no direction… I'm unrecognized… no blood to them… as if our DNA is not eternal… paternal… your backbone was the root that grounded this whole family… weaving in and out connections… pouring her love and affection… making sure everyone walked the straight and narrow path… making sure sins were washed away by holy baths…. Your bath has long been dead for some time and your family runs amuck and mindset is only "everything's mine"… no sharing… no caring… not conversing in the least… no hellos or goodbyes like an eviction on a lease… there'll be no cook-outs… no parties…

no weddings… no tears… no reunion for lost times over years and years…. Your backbone has left me with vultures that rip me at every pain. Just black birds and big wings… nothing remains the same… your backbone has left me like a body without a spine… I have manners and respect so I can't stand up every time. Your backbone has left me… I wish she never would… 'Cause grandma was stern and with her mouth her words stood… I wish she never left me then our family would be good.

After they shut off the lights while many were still conversing, we all just walked out and kept the conversations going in the parking lot. The twins were deciding what to eat. It was too late to be eating for me. I told them to drop me off at the hotel and they could go and do as they pleased. I stayed in the hotel watching lifetime movies. The movies where the woman stays stupid and know that the guy is the killer. I mean how many sign does he have to give you. I was getting in to the movie when my phone rang. It was my mom.

"Hey Tina, how's M-I-Crooked letter...Crooked letter...I... Crooked Letter ... Crooked Letter ... I... Humpback... Humpback... I?"

"Mississippi is fine mama."

"How have you been? I haven't heard from you in a while. I've been worried about you."

I wondered if I should tell my mom about what happened to me at the hospital. We're so close but I know she would tell my pops and that man would be dead. I just didn't know who to tell.

"I'm good. I finished tonight's set and one night to go."

"That's good baby. I'm so proud of you."

"Thanks mama"

"Have you heard from Sara? She called me a couple of days ago and your pops and I went out of town for a spontaneous getaway."

"Yeah, a couple of days ago she was in the hospital."

"Oh Lord, that's why I haven't been able to reach her. How did this happen?"

"You know how and you know by whom."

"Jesus! Is she doing okay now?"

"I don't know. They discharged her and she went back to him. There was nothing I could do."

"She doesn't belong with that man of hers. She's getting in too deep with all of this."

"I know mama. I'm worried about her safety."

I have my own siblings and my focus is on her majority of the time.

"How is Yasmine and the girls? How's Joshua doing in the marines?" I asked.

"Joshua is fine. He just moved up a rank. I'm so proud of him. His son is going to be just like him one day. Yasmine is doing mighty good for herself as well. She got that radio show now. Her girls are getting so big. They are sassy too. I wish you all were close like you all use to be."

"We've grown up too and everyone is just busy."

"You don't ever need to be too busy for family."

"I call them every now and then."

"You need to reach out more."

"Yes ma'am"

She knows everyone lives in different states and we can't always make plans to bond. Joshua's in the military and his deployment is always up in the air. Yasmine is a top radio disc jockey in Atlanta. I just don't have time right now to do anything but nail this audition coming up, get this license and business opened, and keep booking shows. I dared not approach the conversation like that though. One thing about mama, you don't raise your voice and you don't curse in front of her. Mama maybe nice, but once you think you're too old to get knocked down, she will slap the piss out of you and dare you to cry. My only option was to change the subject before we go back and forth any further and I say something I shouldn't.

"Mom, how's Papa?

Papa is what we called our stepfather. He was the only one that stepped up to the plate to raise us anyway.

"He's fine. He doesn't want you to worry about him. He says that he's proud of you as well."

"Don't make me cry."

My papa has been there through it all. Every first moment I had he was there for it.

I walked over towards the room phone and started to order a Reuben panini.

"Hold on ma."

"Yes, I would like to order the Reuben panini with the chocolate cake. Yes, room 412. Okay"

"I'm back"

"Be careful with ordering room service. You know those prices are too high. For that much you could just go buy the food yourself and cook it. We didn't pay for those culinary classes for nothing."

"Yes, I know"

The food came quickly. I walked to the door and tipped the waiter. I was hungry. About the time I finished my food, in walks Daniel and David drunk. We shared a suite. They wanted to dance. I told them that they were drunk and I walked to my room. David followed.

"Where do you think you're going?"

"I'm going with you." He said with slurred speech.

"I'm going to bed so I know that you aren't going with me."

I pushed him out of the doorway and he fell down. He passed out in front of my door. I slammed the door in his face, locked the door behind me, hopped in my bed and went to sleep. I made sure I slept with my gun. I didn't want what happened at that hospital to happen to me ever again. The next day, I was up super early. I always pack my Bible but seldom do I actually read it. Since it was quiet, I decided to read Acts chapter fourteen and fifteen. Mom had picked up a bible study sheet from church and had mailed it to me last month. I had to start a new routine of something. They say if you do something consistently for thirty days then it will become a habit. I'm still waiting on the habit. The twins had slept a total of twelve hours. I mean they had slept the day away. By the time they woke up, I had already eaten breakfast, went out to get my nails done, went on a mini shopping spree and had came back to the hotel. I was in one of those Terry cloth robes that they supply you with my hair wrapped in a towel. They were both hungover. I mixed them up a "How to get out of hell" reverse hangover drink. Oh it worked. Their stomachs might not have liked it but it did its job. We left the hotel at five o' clock. That five pm traffic was the worse. People finally getting off work and rude as hell. I have to remind myself that patience is a virtue and right now I'm not being virtuous. I wanted to curse half of these drivers out. I did them one better and just gave them the finger. For every driver that pissed me off, I mean mugged them. I know that I'm a work in progress. This progress is taking too long. I get back to the club and I'm just ready to do the damn thing. The host introduces me and I'm already walking on stage.

"Thank you guys for letting me come out and bless the mic. It has been an honor to be amongst you guys."

I grabbed the mic on the stand and exhaled.

Wanna Be Heard

I can tell you that I'm a well known poet getting booked state to state, standing in front of millions regurgitating every lyrical poetry I've ate. Consumed... Spitting them out like I was Twista on a rap cipher. I'd be lying in the worst way. I could tell you my words flow like a well trained pianist. Or out of the mouth of Badu and Jill Scott... but my lungs would be suppressing... sweating palms... just stop... I could tell you that I'm well known like Diana Ross and other names. I'm more like the phantom of the opera... Quasimodo... talented but plagued... people love my talents but won't support because it's me. As if my face was marked by the beast... just treason and treachery... I'd love to finally get credit for carving my heart on white sheets or making films out of my erotic mind... putting poetry to fly beats... I'd like to think that one day I'd stand before the crowd and have someone say, what you waiting for? Speak up and say it loud! Make us proud! Bleed your thoughts as if air has not already turned my violet blood red. Now I'm lying on a bed using it as a prop... like a video drama of poetry... the emotions non stop... I'd like to think people would see me for me... An erotic, poetic, jack of all writers who just happens to be all of me... Not the face or skin... ass or titties... but what's within... I don't spit lyrics on stage slaving for approval of an audience as if I was on *Showtime at the Apollo* ... No claps or boos... just me eradicating my heart or setting up for it's vindication... it's justice... it's removal from shackles and chains... I just want to cough up my guts on paper... Let it bleed letters and words... just so people would understand my feelings ... my expressions... my emotions... not just gossip about me like breaking news you just heard...

I waited until the others spoke and then I blessed the mic again.

Ch. 23

Sound Off

There are more people barking the rights of animals than the right to save a child's life as if the price of animals is worth more. More damn animal exploitation on commercials than the talk of our babies going missing as if children don't matter. Babies can't speak for themselves either but you'd rather put a starved dog on tv. What about the millions of malnourished children in the U.S. sitting in blacked out homes crying for love when hate has consumed them? Yeah, you tell us?! We see more feed the children commercials but only on Sunday morning and way past midnight to even give a damn, but animals get primetime. What about our children abducted into thin air? Gone... seems to be forgotten... sold on black markets as sex slaves but you negate that with the countless girls here who degrade their bodies by wearing pretty much nothing. As if you stamped them as the next victim and we're suppose to say nothing?! Young men gunned down where no fathers are in sight... took their hearts and ran out with their lives... trying to pick up spilled blood their father left dripping from stolen hearts as an offering to gangs to become their fathers. What about the lone women engulfed by generational curses and body image disorders that leave their self esteem plastered to the floor... head in toilets... bodies are eye sores or eyes are now punching bags... pussies are drive through windows and we're suppose to deal with it while an animal gets prime time tv. Well you tell me... does hundreds of thousands of dollars that it takes to deliver a child plus the money it takes to rear it worth less than animal cruelty… let's start saving our communities … then that will stop animal cruelty… or let's build foundations of moral institutions and stepping in to reach back and help one… putting up prisons for profit is not going to stop human cruelty to animals … restoring the hearts of people will…

I finished my set and I bowed. I left the club and headed back to the hotel. I had to leave "Dumbo and Earl" because they were too drunk to function. I hoped by the time I got there that they were functional again. Nope, still drunk. If we weren't so close as we are, I would have fired both of them. Since I am starting up, I just let them sleep it off this time. I guess the "Get out of hell free card" didn't hit them hard enough to make them slow down on the alcohol. I walked over to my room, stepping over both of them quietly. I locked my room again. This was starting to become a habit. I've never locked my rooms. I was starting to become paranoid. Even after I got back from Mississippi, I still slept with my gun. Ty and I are suppose to go on a date this weekend. I don't even feel comfortable doing that. When I was all settled in, I decided to catch up on the news and see what was going on in the world. I flipped between NewsOne with Roland Martin and CNN. There had been another unarmed person to die. This time it was a woman about my age. She died in her cell. They suggest it was a suicide. I promise you it wasn't. I mean I'm looking at the photos and from the angles, she did not kill herself. Try again people! Ugh! This makes me so mad to see so many of our young ones and adults in my generation dying of senseless deaths. Every last one of these could have been avoided. Every last one of these deaths could have been handled properly and justly. Instead we have mother's mourning the death of their child. Children not wanting to be kids because of the fear of getting killed by their own race or those cowards (not all of them are cowards to clarify) who hide behind the badge for power. They rehearse the "good ole' days" is what they want back. The good old days were only good for one race lying to themselves to say that they owned this place called

America. When in fact they murdered the people who lived here and took over. You can't say that you found something. How the hell can you find something that was never lost in the first place. This place was right in front of your eyes just like every other part of the world and universe. Nothing is ever lost, you just never noticed it. That is a whole other conversation that I can't keep my mind wrapped around. I mean I just don't get how people feared for their life from a person that's not even stronger than you with no weapons at hand. Oh, they must have feared the voice in the victim. No voice, no justice. Now when I hear someone say they feared for their life, I will know they shot them to shut them up. You feared the truth, the hatred would come out. I lose many Facebook friends for days voicing their stance on those cases. The ignorance is like a smoked cloud. It's like smoking purple haze clouding their judgement. Their hippie parents must have been descendants of racist pigs who stroked their ego too much. I had to quickly turn off the tv. I mean no one's coming up for air for anything. We are all dying mentally. If it's not fear of what if's, it's fear of what to do in the moment. I couldn't think on that anymore. I had to get ready for the suicide prevention event at my alma mater. This was going to be a challenging event. Not only do I have to perform but I have to give a motivational speech on why people should choose life. That part was the hard part. How could I stand in front of so many people telling them to choose life when all I wanted to do was take mine so I didn't have to keep having nightmares of this assault or sleeping with my gun? I was trying to put a speech together for hours and nothing was coming out. I had nothing. Zilch. None. Nada. Nunca. The time going by so fast wasn't helping either. I was crunching for time and I had nothing prepared. I just decided that whatever came out was what I was going to say. I drove on campus and I parallel parked by the arena. The event was being held in the green and gold room inside the arena, first floor. I was nervous. I should have cancelled but I don't make promises that I can't keep. I went in and sat at the table closest to the door.

The host walked up to the microphone and begin speaking.

"Good evening all. It is a pleasure to have this meeting with you. We all need to talk about suicide and how it affects the people around them. The children that come from them and the stigma it leaves behind. I am a survivor. Way back when, I was at a crossroads in my life and I was drowning in my own part and decisions that I made and some I regret. I was raped at a young age by a man who my mom trusted. This happened for four years. He told me that he would kill me if I told anyone about "our little secret". I was young but I knew that this wasn't a secret that I wanted to keep anymore." She said.

She cried.

"I told my mom what was happening. She didn't believe me. She chose that man over her own child. Me! She took a blind eye to me. This "little secret" stayed in that house. One day my mother had came home from work early and she caught this man on top of her thirteen year old daughter, pulled up a chair and watched. She then began coaching him on positions he should try. My mother did this to me! I felt disgusted and embarrassed with myself. Soon after, I had gotten pregnant by this man. My mom, yet again, took his word over mine. He said that it wasn't his. She ripped my clothes off and beat me. Then she let him sodomize me and beat me. I was beaten so bad that I left that place." She said.

There were no dry eyes in that room as she went on with her story.

"I didn't know what I was going to do or where I was going but I left there. A nice young couple spotted me naked in the streets and rushed me to the hospital. I had lost the baby that night. I was so happy to have had that miscarriage. It wasn't that I didn't want kids but I didn't want it with him. That family took me in but the scars were too deep for me. Countless times I tried to commit suicide. Nothing ever did kill me. The gun was fully loaded and no bullets left the chamber. I took a whole bottle of pills but then I got sick and threw it all up. I tried to hang myself with the ceiling fan but it broke. God was really trying to keep me here. I didn't know for what. Well years later, I had graduated high school. I got accepted into Yale. I began my journey as a suicide prevention counselor. I didn't want anyone to go through what I went through. I didn't want anyone to take their life or attempt to take their life. Here I am now with a medical doctorate in psychiatry focusing on suicide prevention and family interventions. I thank you for allowing me to share my story. Enjoy the show." She ended.

Everyone in the room gave her a standing ovation. We were all passing around the tissue boxes and wiping the tears from the corners of our eyes.

The host had introduced me.

"Let's give it up for my fellow psychiatrist turned entrepreneur Christina Sahara Rhodes." She said.

I never liked people using my government name. You never ever hear your full name called unless you are getting in trouble.

"Thank you, I'd like to say that I am honored to be here in front of you guys. Uh, I don't really know what to say."

A man from the audience yelled, "Open your heart and speak."

"Uh ok. Suicide is never the answer. I thank my fellow psychiatrist for sharing her story. You know God can stop many of things from taking your life. Sometimes it is just not your time to die. Uh... Um... We all have done somethings in the past that we aren't happy about. There have been things done to us that we had no control over. When I look in this room, I see overcomers, fighters, forgivers amongst other things. We have a lifetime ahead of us to take back what was taken from us. Whether we made that decision or whether the decision was made for us. There is no excuse or reason to take your life. Think of all the people that are left behind in these times like friends, family, and aquaintances who care for you. We all have to learn to love ourselves. Love the flaws and scars that are embedded, branded deep in us. We cannot change the past. We can only make a better future for ourselves. Just hold on just a little bit longer and I promise you will make it to some balance. The sun will shine again. The rain will stop. You could dance in the rain while the sun is shining and laugh. Enjoy the moment as it is. Push your way through. Never give up on you. Never choose death. Don't take the shortcut. It is harder but more rewarding to choose life and live than to choose death and hurt those who love you. If you say well I don't have anyone who loves me, then be the love you wish to have."

I finished my speech and was very glad I came. It didn't solve the problem going on inside me but it did help me to see things differently. I began my performance after a long exhale.

An Ode To Stop Suicide

Before you try to cancel your subscription to life… letting faith slip away in an instant… trying to give up because your surroundings are unrecognizable … before you cute your lifetime… knives to deep veins… telling yourself this would ease the pain… before you spew out death lines that nobody cares… before you try to tip over that chair… hanging from high ceilings like no one will ever miss you… before you put that gun to your head drunken off poison induced into alcoholic dreams… before you start mentioning that life is not all what it seems… before you open bottles… forcing pills down your passage… let me your gatekeeper… your sane thought… your light in the tunnel… your sign and wonder… your prayer line… your praise report… your cardiologist… before you thought no one cares… pick up your phone… is some Wi-Fi there… before you say goodbye to your future… before the wrong decision is made… can I bless you with words of encouragement today… You are somebody! You mean the world to me! I understand if you open up and empty out your deepest feelings… before you shed one more tear over lost lovers… abusive others… let me tell you how one loved so many others he gave up his own life… before you decide to pull the plug on your life… just one more line left "I love you!" Now get back up and fight!

The crowd clapped and thanked me for the speech. The performance, meh, not so much. I'm not perfect and I kind of stumbled on the words thinking about my own personal life.

Ch. 24

I was so ready to get home and have a conversation with my bed. We haven't been on the same page in a long time. I wanted nothing less than a peaceful, silent night. I cried too much earlier to do anything but be silent. That host's story had me thinking hard on the way home. How God had saved her life all those times and she still made it through to be a successful doctor. I knew I could do the same or so I hoped. I really couldn't sleep that night. I was tossing and turning thinking about that night in the hospital. It was eating at my mind. I should have spoken up. I should have told someone. No one would believe me. He was too friendly at work for anyone to think he was anything less. I cried. I cried hard. Tears were drowning my eyes. Tears were painful. My gut was turning and twisting in knots. I was holding something in that was literally killing me. It was killing my soul. I couldn't stop crying. It was about three in the morning when I called Ty.

"Hello, what's up?"

"Come over"

"You crying?"

"Just come over."

It didn't take long before he got there. He unlocked the door and rushed upstairs.

"What's going on?"

"Hold me"

"Why are you crying?"

"I just need you to hold me."

He took his shoes off and got under the covers with his "black lives matter" shirt and black shorts. He held me tight. He held me close. He ran his fingers through my hair until I fell asleep. It was security that I was looking for. I didn't want to spend another night scared. I didn't want to spend another night sleeping with a gun under my pillow. I wanted to be free but it was going to take more than this man laying next to me for that. He fell asleep shortly after. We both awoke after a nightmare that I was having. He just held me tighter and I cried myself to sleep. The next morning he called in to work because he knew something was going wrong with me. He just felt like he shouldn't leave. I woke up minutes later.

"Hey, how are you feeling?"

"I'm okay"

"We need to talk about last night."

"There's nothing to talk about."

"There is something going wrong with you. You are having nightmares about something."

"It's nothing"

"Look at me"

I looked away.

"Look at me" He yelled.

I looked him in the eyes with all the pain that filled mine.

"What is wrong with you?" He asked.

"It's nothing. I don't want to talk about it."

It wasn't that I didn't want to talk about it. I didn't know how to talk about it. I could help so many people but in this moment I couldn't help myself. How could I tell the man that I'm in love with that someone had sexually assaulted me. Had put his hands where it never should have been. I couldn't do that. I couldn't disappoint him. Later that week, we dressed up and went on a date. He never asked me again about my nightmares but I knew that I was going to have to tell someone soon. Our date that weekend was nothing but blissful. We went to railroad park. We sat out on the grass and listened to the jazz that was playing there. We had brought our own picnic picks. We danced and twirled around like all of the 90s television couples.

Funny they played "My Funny Valentine" and we danced closer. Looking into each other's eyes, it felt as if we were finally looking into each other's souls. Mine was breaking and his was solid. My heart needed repairing. We ended the date laying on the blanket full of collages of our college days. We just laid there looking at the clouds. This day was perfect. This was a start. This day was secure. This day was secured by his protection. We later picked up our things and headed to the car. I told him to stay at my place for a while. I could tell that he wanted to know why but he never asked. We pulled up into my driveway. He got out the car and walked around the front of the car to open my door. He held my hand as I got out. We entered the house. I felt dirty doing anything. Sex seemed to turn me off but with him, sex seemed like my security blanket. I had to hold on to stay safe.

Ch. 25

We ran upstairs to my room and shared the shower. Slowly washing each other's bare bodies we became clean again. I leaned in on my tiptoes and kisses him. With my tongue, I examined his mouth. Our tongues made love in each other's mouth. As we exited the shower and moved towards the bed our bodies made love to each other. They shared the same tune, the same message, and the same synchronised beat. My body ached for his. It needed to feel the security that came with a man who was willing to protect her. I needed him in this moment. His hands began to caress my breasts. The more he slowly pushed inside me, the more these walls closed in on him. We made fire and were consumed by it. We peaked one after the other. Then I looked at the clock and rushed to get back in the shower. Daniel kept blowing up my phone. It kept going to voicemail while I was getting dressed. The next event was being held at Tropic Lounge in Tampa, Fl. The twins never liked to fly unless it was really necessary. Daniel was standing outside my door when I opened it. He grabbed my luggage out of my hands and shoved them in the truck. He had the black Lexus SUV. His vehicles stayed clean. He was really mad at me for not being ready on time. He didn't speak a word the whole drive there. I was unbothered by his childish actions. I had bigger things going on. I leaned my head against the window and watched cars pass us. I watched as some drivers were distracted by eating, drinking, texting, and fussing with their passengers. We passed slowly by a three car pile up. I prayed to myself that God would watch over them. I hoped that I was changing for the better. My life sure wasn't. I stayed up the whole ride there just thinking about life. What I was doing with my life. Was I making the right decisions for my life. I was tired. We made it to the club. I took two shots of patrón and sipped on a long island iced tea before going on stage to perform. I finally felt relaxed enough to perform. The host was a chunky man with the Rasta look. While smoking his blunt standing in his Bob Marly shirt he introduced me. I smiled. I walked to the stage. I closed my eyes and tried to breathe to keep from crying. This was an adult only set and crying and seducing never went together. Unless you cried softly while climaxing during sex, this was not the place to cry. I held back the tears and switched my thoughts to Ty.

The Instructions

I know we've been though this many times before. Here are your instructions for when you walk through the door. I am no longer your wife but your master. Drive to my house going sixty or faster. Strip when you enter. Don't say a word. Crawl to the bedroom like a cat to a bird. There will be three boxes, be careful what you choose. One you're fucking me, one I'm fucking you... this is no rollercoaster... to no time will I amuse... but one card will choose what I'm wearing... trust me, you're only choosing shoes... there's a bathroom for the Jacuzzi and all the pedals and wine... there's my chocolate on a platter where under bubbles you will dine... massaging jets in hot tubs and oils for you to rub... don't think to take your time... there's a whip if you mess up... an evening of punishment... you wouldn't want any other love... so choose your night wisely... but be careful not to rush because time is of the essence and my clock says to fuck you up!

I finished my set and bowed. We didn't stay at a hotel this time. This time we stayed at the twins cousin's house. He had a pool house out back. We were trying to save money. Sometimes we liked to switch it up also. We didn't always stay in hotels. Sometimes we stayed at relatives houses who lived in the city. It was more fun to do so. Food was free. That really is the only line you ever needed to hear.

Ch. 26

On the drive back home we stopped at IHOP for some breakfast. I always got the apple pancakes, three eggs scrambled with cheese, the sausage, and apple juice. Daniel got the western omelette. David got the blueberry crepes, We sat and ate in pretty much silence. We never really said much over food like I did with the girls. After finishing breakfast, we headed back home. I had to rush home, change clothes, and meet David back in his office. I had found a space for my business. The old Continental Ballroom had been shutdown for years. I had so many memories in that place. It was actually the first time I danced with Ty. The parking was good enough for the crowd that I wanted and it was big enough for what I wanted to do with it. There needed to be a permanent business there. There needed to be a place where those of creative minds could go and say whatever. I pulled up in the parking deck, scanned my I.D., and found a parking spot this time on the second floor. I walked to his office off the elevator. I took a seat near the window.

"Hey"

"Hey, so you've found a place?"

"Yes, the old Continental."

"Really? We had so many memories in that place. Man that place was lit back in the day. It would be nice to see it change."

"Yeah, I'm so excited."

"I bet you are."

"I am. I just have to get the permits, the liquor license, the hired security, and the DJ."

"Well I can help you on the license and permits. I will start on those contracts for you as soon as possible."

"Thanks! You know this schedule is jammed packed. I feel like I don't have any real time to rest."

"Isn't it a good thing to be booked?"

"It is but I never thought it would pick up this fast though."

"It's only going to go faster."

"I hope not. I need sleep. A lot of sleep."

"You sleep on the drive to everywhere."

"I need the sleep."

We both shared laughs. I checked my phone for the time.

"Well let me get home because I have to unpack and repack. All of these performances is draining."

"You asked for it. You are living your dreams. Live it happily. Love it peacefully. Always be thankful for where you are now. It's not everyday that people get to have these opportunities. Have you been practicing for your monologue audition by the way?"

"I will."

"It's getting closer to time."

"I know"

"Better get to writing miss thang."

"I will. I will talk to you later tonight."

"Okay and I hope to get right on those contracts and licenses. Have a good day. Try to enjoy the moment."

"Okay, see you later."

"Bye"

His phone rang and he picked it up. I walked out of his office and headed down the elevator to my car. I paid my ticket and drove back home. Thank God that I caught the 65 before the five o' clock, getting off work traffic. I stand by my words every time that no one around here knows how to drive. Too many people are too distracted to drive properly. I headed home rushing again. This time I was rushing for the bathroom. I was doing the potty dance praying that I make it to the toilet before it ran down my leg. I made it. I checked my voicemails. One was from my mother asking me if I was coming home for Easter and if I had read my Bible again. She keeps asking me this. Another was Ty telling me that he was working late. Then there was another one from him saying that he'd be gone for a week on a conference with the other sports medicine doctors. Since he had a doctor's office and not assigned to the hospital, he was a little free with his schedules as far as being on call was concerned. The next event was in Chattanooga, Tennessee. I was performing at the Barkingaleg Theatre on Dodds Avenue. I packed an overnight bag. We booked the hotel with the train sitting on top of it. It was quite interesting to say the least. We plugged in the GPS and it helped us find the place. We almost got lost twice. Sometimes I wonder if the GPS systems don't update closed roads or roads that are no longer there on purpose to make people look stupid. I did the same routine here as the last. I downed two shots of patròn and sipped my long island. This host was more easier on the eyes. This time I was suppose to perform with no other performers in between. I had the stage all to myself. I didn't know what Daniel had up his sleeve but I wish he had told me that I was going to be performing all by myself way before we got here and not minutes before I'm suppose to perform. Thank God I had all the pieces that I wanted to perform already rehearsed. This time I had to do them back to back. There was no break time anymore. The stage was all mine. I got called on stage and I performed the heck out of my set.

"Thank you all for having me come out. I didn't know that I had you all to myself until just now. Be patient with me."

I settled in. I took a deep breath. I took another shot of whatever it was the bartender gave me and performed.

"This one is called "Scoreboards". I hope you like it"

Scoreboards

Looking through newspapers... never would have expected editors to be so heartless... so deceitful... using the slain blood of our deceased boys as scoreboards on front pages like this was something to sit in stadiums... eating heart attacks... keeping tally for every strike, strikeout, and homerun that stuck guns to innocent children... civilians... bystanders... going about their everyday lives only to be forced in an integrated league of baseball set up for failure and the pitcher has a gun instead of a ball... shooting at heads of black genes... forcing "ball" but they never make it to base one because the catcher holds body bags instead of gloves... more like catching fallen out... just knocked cold bodies as if they were ushers in the church... so now the streets are graveyards... and the only dream far out is graduating... every year... every month... pulling out scoreboards of dead and wounded black children like strikes and homeruns... crucified to the streets... the same people that followed them.... or ones who made an oath to protect them now betray them like Judas... yeah, he hung himself... couldn't face spilled blood on his hands... so when you see my children's death posted up like scoreboards, speak up!... this is not a baseball game ... don't let them throw bullets yelling "ball" at my innocent to now dead bodies to be caught by body bags ... so when you see the scoreboards, speak up!... this is not a game... no one's making it to base one... back home... streets are now graveyards... nothing's changed...

Ch. 27

This one is called "Still Here".

Still Here

To be so blinded by invisible racism… denying that the sins of the father still exists… sweeping ideologies and hardened slave master mentalities under rugs… well it's basically on the bottom of magic carpets flying right above us… right above what we want to see … looking ahead but we all know the psychological dysfunction of equality and justice is like a short nightmare… a gaze… an absent seizure… unaware of the world… and just like that… a voice with that mindset just regurgitated… so you can taste the acid on his words… that it burns through your ears like hot lava erupting out of the head of a volcano…. And it stated, "All blacks need not be in high offices. They belong on plantations as slaves" and that was the comment of a senator member today and we're too blinded to see the destruction… we're so much like Israel given so many chances and yet wallowing in their eternal invaluable items… worshipping Baal gods that won't save them… blinded too deep as if our retinas were shot…can't understand… comprehend that it only takes one 2/3 vote to go back to shackles and pig Latin… broken English… hidden dialects… so to save our own selves…see we were once in high places… then chained like sub-humans living in a dire circumstance of inadequacy… never measuring up… scapegoats to infidelities and other incriminating acts… then somewhat back in high places making meaningless pacts to enlighten others... my sisters and brothers... but one 2/3 vote and history repeats... men dominating in white sheets... more like behind badges... homeland of genocides... through our absent seizure eyes and we stare out of our own bodies... telling yet another lie... racism is abolished... dismissed...

There was an intermission for everyone to use the bathroom or grab a drink for the bar. Many of the audience was my age or in college.

I took a sip of water and went back in my zone.

"This next one is called "I Just Need You".

I Just Need You

Sometimes I need to have you lift me up... hold my pain upon your back and carry me... Sometimes I need to be able to trust you enough to give me the encouragement to strengthen myself... I just need to rest on your broad shoulders and reach for the Holy Spirit to pierce through my heart to yours... I just need to be lifted up and held... mounted on my patriarchic totem pole and covered with protection to only be seen and not touched... not harmed... just lifted upon your arms...

Ch. 28

I was getting tired but I had one more piece left to perform. This piece I wrote when Ty and I had that fight. We stopped talking for a while.

"This piece is called "Tell me you hate me". Sometimes you're in a relationship with someone that is an up and downhill battle. Sometimes you argue and sometimes you both split. Well someone's going to keep the feelings. I just want you to be straight with me with your feelings. Just blatantly tell me you hate me so that I could move on. Don't ignore me then sell me a dream of reconciliation. Just for once don't let me hang off a bridge trying to pull me up and drop the rope at the same time. Just tell me how you feel point, blank, period. That way we can both move on and no one is looking stupid or lost. Well if this sounds like you, then this is for you.

Tell Me You Hate Me

Can you do me one favor? Just tell me that you hate me so my heart can unplug from the pacemaker. Tell me you never loved me so I can stop having that machine breathe for me. Watching my lungs rise and fall... crying for every day you never called... Tell me there was no connection. Tell me I never felt your affection. Quality time was a mirage centered on what I dreamed it to be. Tell me to leave you alone. Let there be no assumptions... Since I cried, shedding waterfalls for nights, and I'm left to wonder when you will ever just push me away. Say no... Just tell me that you hate me! Speak the words so I can go. Freefall... give up... stop dreaming of the girl we wanted to have… oh in my dream, her name was Jessica. It doesn't matter… it will never happen… Just tell me you never felt me. It was just a mask. Tell me that you hate me so the pain can finally pass.

When I had finally finished the whole set. The audience clapped and I bowed. It felt good to not be able to share the stage with other people. I missed sharing the stage with other people. It felt really good to fly solo. I had another long eventful night coming. I called Ty on the way home. He didn't answer. Ten minutes later he called me back.

"Hello"

"Hey, I haven't heard from you in a while and I was calling to see how you were doing?"

"I'm good. I'm kind of busy though. Why? What's up?"

"Uh … Umm … Do you love me?"

"You know how I feel about you."

"That's not what I asked though."

"Look I'm busy. Can we talk about this when I get off?"

"Whatever"

I hung up the phone without even saying goodbye.

Sometimes you just want a man to say it and act on it. I guess he was too scared to do so. When I got home there were flowers at my doorstep. I thought it was from Ty but it was from the assaulter. I quickly threw them in the trash can. I didn't even bother to read the card. It had his name on the outside. I ran inside my house and locked the doors. I slept with the gun under my pillow again. Late in the night Ty had came over. He crawled up in my bed trying to wake me. There were no lights on. I woke up startled and reached for my gun.

"Get out!"

"What?"

"How'd you get in here?"

"I got a key."

I took the safety mode off my gun and cocked back the chamber.

"Get the hell out!"

"It's me"

"What?"

Ty quickly ran to turn the lights on.

"What the hell Ty? I could have killed you."

"What the hell is what I should be asking you? Put that thing away before you actually kill someone."

I put the safty more back on and put it in my drawer.

"What is wrong with you? You've been acting strange for a month now."

"It's no--"

"Don't tell me "It's nothing". Something is definitely wrong with you."

I knew I couldn't keep it a secret anymore. I told him what had happened at the hospital. He was livid. He began pacing the room like a mad man.

"I'm a kill him! Where is he?"

I started crying all over again.

"I don't know. Please don't do anything stupid."

"No!"

I knew I should have kept that to myself. It was my battle anyway. I patted the bed.

"Get in."

"Let me think for a minute."

He sat down on his side of the bed. He grbbed my hand, kissed my forehead, and pulled me closer to him.

"Why didn't you tell me this before? I love you!"

"I love you too. I was disappointed in myself for this."

"There is no reason to be disappointed in yourself. You did nothing wrong. That sick bastard was the foul one."

I just layed on his chest and cried.

I didn't tell him about the flowers. He was already mad. I didn't tell him the whole story. He couldn't handle it if I did. The next few days were testy. If I woke up in the middle of the night screaming, Ty would jump up locked and loaded and ready to shoot. I had a long weekend ahead of me too. It just seemed like everything was going by so fast. The next event was back at the Soul Wired Cafè in Jackson, Mississippi.

Ch. 29

This time the club was more intimate. I walked in and I knew there were new bouncers at the door. I have never been accused of not being me. Yes, I probably needed to update my license due to the weight loss. I still look the same people. The Rastafarian host called me up to the stage then farted. I passed out. Thank heavens for the ammonia under the nose trick. He knew he was wrong for that with his stanky ass. When I stood up, he was laughing. He whispered how I was such a weakling. Don't anyone I know wanted to smell something that ferocious. It literally comatosed my senses. They all blacked out at once. That was foul and he knew it.

"Yeah, excuse me for fainting but "bruh man" over there put my whole senses in a coma for a couple of seconds. Whole system shutdown. Hold up! Let me regroup. Dann! In my face, dude!"

They laughed. I took a deep breath. Paused. I began performing.

"This first one is called "When Our Paths Cross".

When Our Paths Cross

That awkward moment when our paths cross and I'm just speechless with my head down… I know I should be happy, but I can't seem to find it when I've lost my crown. I know we all take different paths. Some shorter than others… Sometimes I regret mine. Sometimes I pity yours. Sometimes I envy others. Sometimes I think it would be better if my path was erased. My being was untraced.

That I no longer existed and then I look at the past… I can't find the light to smile for your success knowing mine is nonexistent and I look at traffic wanting to just walk in it and become missing. When our paths cross, I hold my head down. I can't seem to smile. My world is upside down. Beating myself up over endless mistakes and things I had no control over… When our paths cross and my head is down, know that I'm proud of your path and your achievements but I just can't say it right now. When our paths cross and my head is down, just say hi with a smile. Tell me that I will make it. Open a door instead of looking down the bridge of your nose… I am still human. When our paths cross and my head is down, just speak life instead of gossip. Make me smile instead of cry. Tell me weeping may endure for a night but joy, oh joy, comes in the morning. When our paths cross and my head is down, just hug me, say nothing negative, and pray until you see my crown.

I took some small breaths.

"This next one is called "Unison?"

Unison?

If the world was in unison like our blood is then we'd never have to be taught different based on race and safety. Looking out, survival is taught differently and my heart wishes our minds bled like our veins. The same oxygenated blood spilling out our bodies like hot geysers and I wish… I wish our children wouldn't be taught to hate. Discriminate… Spew out regurgitated death in the power of their tongues out of their hearts. The mouth speaks. It can either bless or kill you. Put a death sentence like snake venom… I wish our mind would be in unison with our blood. That it all bleeds the same… That no child or human being would be taught to call another out of their given name… If we were all in unison then how would the game change?

There was a twenty minute intermission. I guzzled a whole bottle of water. I took it to the head like vodka. We all mixed and mingled with each other. I looked at the clock and headed back to the stage.

"Thank you for your patience. This next piece is called "If To Wonder".

If To Wonder

If to wonder if you're over where you are wondering about me... if you're thinking did I miss her... Or will one day she'll up and leave... Or if you're thinking no one could love you so she must be lying... Keeping silent how you feel while her heart is symbolically dying... If you're wondering if you still knew what her voice sounds like... If you still knew what made her comfortable at night... wondering if she's moved on because you were to shy or prideful to step up... Wondering if you'll ever find another lover... well if you have to wonder so much and it's ripping at your heart... Just take the first step and say it... speak and sew back up your heart... It only takes one time to make the fire start, just don't let it die and fall apart...

"This next piece is called "Who Taught You To Hate Yourself?".

Who Taught You To Hate Yourself?

The misconception of beauty has been cloned too many times. At first the culprit was pointing back into our psyche. Our psychological is branded into our personality... our frontal cortex... that no matter what we did, it was only "Good enough for a darky"... "Good enough for a woman"... "Good enough for a black person"... but why not good enough as a human? I am that first and foremost you know or don't you understand! Who gave you the right to engrave your venomous thoughts upon my siblings, my brethren, and my sister's mind that it's just good enough for a ---... I look countless times over at my strong sisters at on time branded in their psyche that light skin was better... that curly hair was better... that big hips and full ass... double D's and a mouth to please a man was considered so much better. The total package... well physically... but who gave you the right to hate yourself? Push the concept that all of the above was better. Devalue your identity because magazines don't recognize the diversity of true beauty. You hide your natural roots growing from your head masking it with the roots stolen off another sound asleep in their bed. Paying prices above your means to get the satisfaction, the pseudo confidence to look in the mirror and say "I am beautiful!"... Who gave you the right to hate yourself? I see too many young lost girls conditioned into being this desired weight that they live in toilets, have snakes constrict them at their throats so they painfully regurgitate fear and low self esteem. Conditioned to be a certain weight for different sports, they too forget that they are human. Their health comes first. Who gave you the right to hate yourself? Crushed down by adults living vicariously through you and your soul suffers. Yes, I see so many other girls, young women, grown women living out of their pussy like it was the only thing they had to justify security. Control... baby daddy after baby daddy... Oh he loves me, they say.... He's not like the last one, they say... He's changed, they tell themselves... Burned words have no meaning and you can crumble them from ceilings and let their ashes be quicksand slowly pulling you deeper in until you suffocate on your vomit and die. Who told you to hate yourself? Who gave you the right to devalue yourself that much? Hate is always taught, never birthed and I'd be damn if I let it consume my sisters on this earth opening their pussy like broken ATM's letting every man take the value out. I refuse to be a bystander watching my sisters lay heads upon toilet seats bleeding tears upon regurgitated acid conditioned to be this deadly weight and covering it up with signs that say "Perfect". I refuse to let my sisters dehumanize, murder their identity selling it off to high bidders because the world is colorblind, texture blind. Blinded to never see that all are naturally beautiful and they shine without remorse. And a bright personality and education... dreams lived out... is what matters most under the most high... Just those conditions of hatred, generation against generation, light versus dark, curly versus kinky, mirage of perfect versus healthy need to go on and die out. Stop living vicariously through our daughters! Teach them that beauty is in everyone. Teach them that no one is perfect. A perfect weight is a dead weight. The hair on your head is beautiful. God didn't make one thing he hated. Who gave you the right to hate yourselves? Dehumanize yourselves? Exploit yourselves? Devalue yourselves? That's nothing but demonized oppression covering you. Suppressing your glory… When you think to hate your flaws, we all have them. When you think to hate your hair, trust me, there's always something we can learn to do to love it. When you think to devalue yourselves, it's not worth it. Letting men keep your souls hidden in their mouth or pulling them out by chains clamped to their dicks… When you think to exploit yourselves, just stop! Nothing ever stays a secret. When you think to dehumanize yourselves, you are somebody. First and foremost, you are human. You are not just good enough for a (Name Your Stereotype). You are at best because you are human. When you think to hate yourself, don't you dare! Who the hell gave you that right?!

"I won't keep you that much longer. This last piece is called "Let It Happen".

Let It Happen

Learning to never wait for an absent person… I am just here. Smiling to the heavens… Erasing tears like chalk on chalkboards… Driving my nails across it to get your attention but you cover your ears and never listen. You never look up. Never notice the reason why you feel… Sometimes I'd like to tell you the reason no girl is working out is because you have already found the one. "Not rushing" is an excuse because you don't want to admit that love is set and stone and you have already been chosen. Destiny is waiting yet you're too cautious to see. Live and love is birthing out of me. Reaching out to you… Thinking no one could ever love you yet running from the one that does. Just relax… Release and let love capture thee. Consummate and all consuming bond that strikes fire like the forest but is as beautiful as the northern lights… Let me plow the wind into your passage. Secure your last feelings… Let doubt be step stools as we break through glass ceilings and you tell me you love me and mean it. And life finally goes on with no regrets…

I finally got to breathe. I bowed and thanked the people for bringing me out. I was headed home and oh so tired. It seemed like I had been going non-stop. When I finally got home, I thought I could rest. That was not going to happen. I got another call from Sara. I thought what is it now?

Ch. 30

"Hey Tina, I'm in trouble"

"Hey, did he hurt you?"

I knew I was asking the most dumbest question in this case.

"I need you to come over please." She begged.

Her voice started to tremble. I knew something was serious.

"He's going to kill me" Hurry, I don't want to die." She cried out.

"Where are you? Did you call the police?" I asked.

"I -- I -- I'm locked in the bathroom with my kids. They wouldn't come. He's going to kill me. I -- I -- I have to go." She said.

Once again I was on my way to fight. I had a short fuse. I go crazy over the people I love but I can't protect my own space. How ironic?

"Sara?! Sara?!"

I heard the dialtone. Something was going on. I jumped in my car with my gun in my pants. I drove like a madwoman trying to save the day. I should have left it up to the police but I had to be there for her. It was draining me but I had to be there. I arrived at her place. I used my key to open the door. I heard screaming. I followed the sounds in the house to the living room which was around the back past the stairs.

"Sara!" I whispered.

I walked to the living room. Thomas had a gun to her head.

"Sara, are you okay?"

She was on her knees all bloodied up. Her shirt was ripped open. She was pretty much naked on her knees with a .38 at her temple.

"Get the kids!" She yelled.

"Get the fuck out my house!" Thomas said.

"I'm not leaving without Sara and the kids."

"Why do you always have to do this?"

I ignored him.

"Sara!" I cried out.

He clapped.

"Congratulations on your award for "Captain Save A Ho". She doesn't need saving. You can take your saddity ass back to your fancy house and leave me and mine alone."

"Like I said --"

He pistol whipped me in front of her.

I pulled out my own gun.

"Sara!" I screamed.

"Please, just get the kids!" She pleaded.

"I said, get the fuck out my damn house." He said.

"I'm not going anywhere till I know that they are safe." I replied.

He cocked his gun back and I did the same. Eyes locked on each other. If he wanted me out, he was going to die with me.

"Just get the kids. They're in the room." Sara said.

"I can't just let you die." I said.

I knew it was like playing Russian roulette with their lives. Eventually I would have to choose between the lives of my godchildren and one of my best friends. I did not want to make that choice.

"You want me to show you that she's fine so you can leave?"

He pressed against her cheeks so that her mouth opened then kissed her violently. He then turned his gun on me while massaging her clitoris under her shirt.

"See how she's looking at me? She's fine. Go bitch!" He yelled.

I ran for Sara and tried to move his hands and he back handed my face. The loud smack as his hand hit my face grew my rage. Sara knew it too. I had to think clearer and ultimately choose.

Ch. 31

I walked into the room where the kids were. The minute I was out of the sight of the living room, I heard two gunshots. I feared the inevitable. I tried to wake the kids but they wouldn't budge. I check their pulse and found none. That's when I knew they were already dead. I screamed. I called 9-1-1.

"9-1-1 operator, Can I help you?"

"I need an ambulance at 215 Hardy Dr."

"What's your emergency?"

"There's been a shooting. I heard two gunshots and I was headed to the kids room and they're both dead. I checked for a pulse and they both have none. Please send help! Oh My Gosh!" I cried out.

I was crying hysterically by then. Sitting on the floor between the children's room, I cried. I knew I had to eventually go back in the living room to see what had happened. Stumbling over my own feet, heart racing, I walked into the living room. What I saw was the worst nightmare ever. Thomas was laying on the floor in a pool full of blood. His brains were splattered all over the floor. I believe I stepped on a little membrane trying to see the whole picture. Sara's body was naked and her body too was laying in a pool of blood. I seen her lifeless. I cried so heavily. I started to hyperventilate. I just held her body and cried. As much as I was crushed in the moment, I still held my best friend.

"I'm sorry Sara that I didn't choose you. You were my best friend. Sisters for life." I said. I kept crying.

The cops came later. They started taking pictures of the crime scenes. Some walked into the bedrooms and started taking pictures of my babies laying lifeless in their beds. They started carrying the bodies out. They started with the children. One by one they rolled them out zipped up in the black bags. They then got Thomas's body and rolled his dead body out. They came back for Sara's body but I was not ready to let go.

"Ma'am we have to do our job."

"Sara! No! Sara! Why'd you have to die?"

I held her lifeless body tighter. I didn't care if her blood was on my hands. It was her blood. It was apart of her body. In that moment I was still closer to her.

"Ma'am let go" The officer forcefully said.

"Please, five minutes. I just need to hold her. I just need to be near her. Please!" I begged.

The police officers stepped back. You could hear someone clearing their throat as if they were trying not to cry.

I rubbed her hair. I cried. I screamed. I cried harder. I cried like it was the start of the downfall of Rome.

"Sara! Sister! I should have tried harder to protect you. I -- I -- I should have --."

"Ma'am you have to let go." The officer stated.

I just wanted to keep stalling. I just didn't want it be over. Not like this. It hurt. It hurt like hell. Did I really just reach hell at this point? It felt like it.

I got up and stepped aside to let them do their job. They began asking me questions.

"Ma'am how did this happen?" The officer asked.

"I was coming home from my tour. I came home and she had called me panicking about how he was going to kill her. I got in my car and rushed over here."

I started crying again.

"Then what happened ma'am?"

"I unlocked the door with my key and I walked to where she was. She was on the floor with a .38 to her head. She kept telling me to go get the kids but I didn't want to leave her. It didn't feel right. Her husband and I argued."

"What did you both argue about?"

"He wanted me to leave and I wasn't going to without Sara or the kids."

"Then what happened?"

"I had to make a decision to save my best friend or her kids. I chose the kids because that's what she wanted. It was the hardest decision that I had to make. I left the room that's when I heard two gunshots. I kept walking towards the kids and that's when I found out that they were dead."

"Backtrack, why didn't you see what had happened after you left the living room?"

"I thought maybe she stood up for herself. She wanted me to get the kids so I kept her word. When I noticed the kids were dead I cried then went back to the living room and saw what you saw. I dropped to the floor and cried and held my best friend. That was the last time that I would ever be able to be close to her."

I started hyperventilating again.

"Ma'am you need to breathe."

I took deep breaths and I calmed myself down.

"That's when you all came in."

"Is that all?" The officer asked.

"That's all I have." I said.

They handed me their card to call if I had any more information to give. I walked to their pictures and cried. I called Ty.

"Hello"

"Ty, something happened."

"What's going on Tina?"

I cried.

"Why are you crying?" He asked.

"Sara's dead. The kids are dead."

"Where are you?" He asked.

"I'm at Sara's place."

"I'm on my way."

I cried harder. We hung up. I just walked around because I just didn't want to leave her place. I felt like if I did that I would be leaving her.

Ch. 32

I called my mom.

"Hey baby, it's late."

I began crying again.

"What's wrong?"

"Sara's dead. The kids are dead. Thomas is dead."

It was total silence.

"Mom?"

"Oh God! Why?" She screamed.

"Mom?"

"How did this happen?"

"I -- I--"

Nothing would come out. I couldn't find the words to tell anyone.

"I should have saved her. I should have tried harder. I should have pulled the trigger."

"Baby, we not talking about killing anyone."

"I should have been there. It hurts so bad."

"Baby, that pain is going to hurt. I don't know how to ease your pain. I definitely would if I could."

"I can't bring them all down there. I can't."

"Don't worry about that right now."

"I just lost my best friend."

"I know baby."

I hung up when Ty got there. He had his friend drive my car back to my place. Ty was suppose to drive me home as well.

"Ty, I'm glad to see you."

He pulled me closer and I cried on his chest.

"It's going to be okay. Let's go."

"I can't!"

"It's not healthy for you to stay here baby."

"I can't leave Sara. She needs me. Sara! We were suppose to be here together. Sisters for life!" I cried out.

"You have to let go Christina. Sara's gone now."

"It hurts so bad."

"I know. I know."

"Why did this have to happen to her?" I said while hitting his chest.

"I don't know. There are just somethings that we just cannot control."

"I should have killed him."

Ty stepped back and looked at my face. That's when he noticed the bruise after I pushed my hair out of my face.

"What happened to your face?" He asked.

"Thomas pistol whipped me."

"He did what? Where is he? I should kill him right now?"

"No use. You can't kill someone who's already dead." I said sarcastically.

"We really have to get you out of here."

"I can't leave!"

"Why can't you?"

"I should have been there for her. I should have protected her. When he pulled that gun on me and I the same, I should have shot him right then."

"He did what!" Ty yelled.

"I can't just leave this place. Look down! There is still apart of her here."

I pointed down at the blood and brain matter.

Ty tried to pull me away from her place. The more he tried to pull me away, the more I kept running back in the house. He finally had to pick me up over his shoulder and carry me out. That was the worst that he had seen me. He took my keys for her place and locked up after he had buckled me in the car. I cried leaving her place. I finally just cried myself to sleep in his car. I didn't know when I got home but I woke up in my bed. I shortly fell back asleep. The next time I woke up screaming.

"Sara! I'm coming! Don't leave me!"

I cried.

Ch. 33

I didn't know how to process this. I didn't know how to walk away from years of a close relationship. We've been friends since we were eight years old. I had called the family up to Birmingham for the funeral. We had set the date for April 10, 2015. They all stayed at my house around the mountain. Ty stayed at my place as well even though my parents didn't agree. He's truly my strength in all of this. The next weekend we all had fixed ourselves up for her last ride home. I wanted to make her home going special along with her kids. I didn't really care about Thomas. His family held a separate funeral. We lined up to walk through the chapel. I couldn't even look at the casket without crying. All I wanted to do was run to it, grab her body again and cry. I held my composure. My mother grabbed hold of me. I rested my head on Ty's shoulders and cried. As I looked around while the preacher began. I had seen Brittani and Natalie who were siting behind me. Daniel and David were sitting two rows behind me. Jennifer was nowhere in sight. We were all close or so I thought. Why wouldn't she show up when she said that she was going to be here? She never came. I wanted to give a speech but my voice failed me yet again. It has became a habit of it not wanting to speak. We played the slideshow that I put together of all of us supposed friends. They wheeled her body out and I ran out of the chapel and to my car. I didn't want to see her being buried. I didn't want to say goodbye. The repast was at my house. There was so much food there. People came up to me with their condolences.

"I'm sorry you had to go through this Tina. I know you were closer to her. I wish there was something that I could have done more." Natalie said.

"I try to ask myself that every day."

"Well at least she's in a better place." Natalie said.

I never liked when people said that as if not living on this earth with her kids and friends wasn't better.

"Yeah" I said and walked away.

"I don't know what to say Tina. Your mom called me and told me. I didn't know what words I could say if I called you. I should have done something." Britt said.

"Yes, just you being here is good for me. I was not in the right state of mind to take calls that night." I said.

"Where's Jennifer?" Britt asked.

"I don't know. She wasn't at the funeral either. I looked for her." I said.

"The only person that Jennifer wakes up and goes to sleep thinking about is herself." Britt said.

I really didn't want to gossip. I just wanted this day to be over with so that I could rest and go back on my tour. My mom walked over and wanted to talk.

"Can I steal her for a minute Brittani?" Mom asked.

"Sure" Brittani replied.

She grabbed my hand and we walked out back to the patio. She gave me this letter that was addressed to me.

"An officer dropped this off yesterday. He said that he found it at Sara's place while they were trying to piece together what happened last week. I hope you find comfort in it." She told me.

It was from Sara. She had this silly slanted writing when she wrote my name. It was our thing when addressing each other on paper. We started this back in high school. I didn't want to open it right then. I just wanted to cherish it because these were her lasts words and thoughts. It made me smile.

"Thanks for this. I really needed this."

"Maybe now you can get closure. You can finally, slowly but surely, let go."

Everyone knows that closure is a myth. It's a hallucinative thought. It's torture. It's a mirage. Closure doesn't exist in life. You move on but the pain never leaves. You find the strength to keep living. You push your pain through. Closure is like fibromyalgia. Everyone can see how strong you are moving forward on the outside, but not the fact that you're dying internally. No one sees the nightmares at night. They don't see how things could trigger pain with just a word, another person's story, or their favorite thing. Closure does not exist.

"What if I don't want to?"

"Not now, but one day you will."

We both ended in silence and starred at the sky as if that sign of rain coming down was either the start to closure or just the start of pain. Shortly after, the crowd left my house and it was just my mother, Ty, and I.

I had to get up though and fight. I had taken a break from my tour for far too long. Missed dates was missed money. I was not going to sit in this house and lose sleep anymore.

Ch.35

I took two more days off my tour to clear my head. When I was ready, I called Daniel and told him to let the bookers know that the show will go on. I packed my bags. I looked at the letter from Sara and quietly whispered, "Sisters for life". Daniel was knocking on my door like he was beating on the drums.

"Stop knocking on my door like that! I'm coming." I yelled.

I walked downstairs with my bag in tow. We were headed back to Atlanta. This segment was like erotic poetry and that other kind. Erotic poetry was my favorite. I didn't have to be real. I could be seductive. I could be alive. I could be imaginative. It was an escape to ecstasy. We got in the car and loaded up. We both buckled our seatbelts because now the cars won't start unless you do. It didn't take us long to get there. We were back at ILounge for the "Don't You Tell" edition. I was flying solo again. Daniel told me that I'd be flying solo in these tours from here on out. That means I have the stage all night. That also means my feet are going to hurt if I dress sexy. High Heels and performances don't mix if it's long. I walked in the club and sat closer to the bar as the audience was still walking in. Their host was fine as hell for this session. He was tall, caramel skin with green eyes and a clean beard. I had to stay focused. My attention drifted after I noticed the black diamond wedding ring. I knew he was too good looking to be single. He walked on stage and introduced me as the lady love. I smiled and winked as I walked on stage.

"Thank you guys for having me out tonight. I hope I rock your world. This first piece is called "Hold Me."

Hold Me

Hold me in your heart so I cannot fall against my will. Let the river of life overshadow my pain so that if I tilt, I shall fall in your embrace and never face the thought and fear that this is love, oh so sacred bond was a waste. I'd play in your ever so faithful realms and kiss stars plucked out of the sky, plugged into my wall, just to see glow upon me. As if there never was a tomorrow and the only thing I feared was tonight. Tuck me under your protection and do not harm my delicate heart. For it tells the story to my spirit and my soul overhears it that you are accountable and faithful, and ever true and strong. Hold me up past a lifetime lying safely in your arms.

They clapped.

"This next piece is called "Who says?"

Who Says?

Who says I can't be anything but the color of my skin? As if my skin was just a stereotype mixed with phenotypes and genotypes. Who says I can't be natural? I was born that way you know! Molded into society and fictitious social idiocies wrapped in plastic… shown in cages like Sara… Turned away from my own skin as if it was the young girl saying the white doll was prettier. Forced to lie to peers about above average grades to fit into the normalcy of teenage mothers and dead brothers' spilled blood in the streets… Assassinated by wanna be thugs who never knew what love was. Who says I can't be different? Formed and striped to believe that reality TV is success. Not buying that! A fool ain't successful airing out their own mess! Tell me who says I can't be the best! What's the best to you? I know I am better and my words are stamped with truth. Who says that the standard of beauty is what another woman's body is? Baby, genetics ain't make me identical to her! Beauty is what I say I am! Who says that all I am is a mad black woman? Well that's far from the truth. If you push the issues past my morals and beliefs, my words will cut you like a two-edged sword. I'll promise to bring the alcohol for your open wounds. Tell me who says I can't! I can show you "can't" was never born. This is all natural, baby! I'll take your "can't" set on fire like a woman scorned.

They clapped. It was less claps this time.

"This last piece is something I know you all came for. This one is called "Storm".

Storm

The night was dim. Lit up by lightening… Felt like its rods had struck your stick shift… The inclination of your thrust sliding deeper up and down hills of my garden… between sheets we made the sounds of music… We rehearsed *Birth of a Nation*. I scratched up your car with my nails on chalkboards and you were hypnotized by my chocolate covered cherry between my thighs making you realize that I was the thunder moaning. Falsetto of my vibrato as I vibrated on second gear and your eyes shed tears like it had been in droughts for years. I kissed it like dew in the morning and you started coming and my thunder got louder. Your lightening touched down deep in my rivers. My tornadoes erupted and covered your lightening forming from our hurricanes and we rested on the seventh day. I snuck back into the storm to get another taste, but you were sleep and not ready. I stole you and took over and you whimpered as your lightening got stronger till my tornadoes covered your lightening. We rode the earth like a super cell destroying every habitat till you fell into a coma and I sucked you dry.

I bowed. The crowd cheered. I thanked them again for letting me come out. I didn't mingle this time because I had to get back in time to get some sleep, repack, and be at Shuttlesworth Airport at six in the morning. We were headed to Philly for the "Don't Ask, Don't Tell" cocaine shots series. This was my favorite series ever. I was only performing one of them though. We were going to be at the G-Spot Soul Food Café. It always stays buck wild when we do these series. If you've never been to a cocaine shots series then you are totally missing out. I only do these once a year. Still I have to explain that cocaine shots are not about drugs, they're about sex. Sex is a drug so I guess I should stop explaining. Phone rang. I looked down and it was mom.

"Hey mom"

"Hey, I was just calling to see how you were doing."

"I'm fine. I'm back on tour again. I'm making my dreams come true."

"Don't you think you need to slow down? You've been through so much."

"I need to work mama. Slowing down is torture. Slowing down is having to sit down and actually think about it all. It's not healthy for me to rehearse this everyday."

"You are jumping into work too fast. That is all I'm trying to say."

"Goodbye mom"

"Don't hang up on me!"

I hung up anyway.

I know she means well but the more I stay still, the more I process and rehearse the whole nightmare. I just need a getaway in my mind. It needs to think on something else. My work does that for me.

Ch. 34

We caught our flight and headed out to Philly. I always had gum on deck to keep my ears from popping in the plain. Daniel was the fear of flying one. I mean we have been on planes all this time and yet he still throws up when we get up in the air. Sometimes I make him take a sleeping pill so it won't be so bad on him. You'd think this would be one thing he would grow out of right? Wrong! I doubt he will ever grow out of this fear. I mean who has a fear of flying but will still fly. We arrived safely in Philly and instead of booking a hotel; we stayed at my cousin's rental property. It had more of a contemporary setting. We all unpacked and relaxed. David had went out and bought more groceries. I don't see why since the refridgerator was more than overstocked. I was practicing this long ass piece. We had to break it up just to fit the time slot. We made sure that the security was deep. I didn't want to be approached by randoms again. It was about five in the afternoon when we left headed out to the club. We arrived in about an hour due to traffic. It was a really great turnout. The host was a vertically challenged woman with a pixie cut and a short, fitted red dress. She was the color of black castor oil. Her hair was as radiant as the sun. Her sister locks looked great on her. Her name was Imani. When she introduced me, I felt her hand going down my backside. I had girls crush on me but damn. Expect nothing when coming to these series. Everything and anything happens. The last time I had this series, I could have sworn I seen Pandora opening her box to a train of guys. I walked to the stage.

"Thank you all for bringing me back. It's good to be back in Philly. I hope your eyes roll back, your toes curl, and I leave you satisfied."

I pulled the chair closer to me that they had prepped on stage for me. I motioned for a chocolate man with long dreads mid back length. He had deep brown eyes. His muscles were like Samson's. I pushed him back in the chair once he got on stage. Then I began to slowly untie my robe and drop it.

Cocaine Shots

The door creaks and I hear it. The sax playing in the background and I'm sitting in a tub of lavender all wet now. Rosè down my chest... massaging rosè like ex between lips of Pandora and my legs quiver at the thought of you as I get ready. Hot vanilla bean oils slipping down my Double D's; forty two to be exact... I ease out of the rose covered tub. Slip into silk lingerie... Diamond heels on... Click... Click... Thinking of your dick... Asking how the conversations would be to see my clit pulsate and erupt cocaine shots on your tonsils and have you swallow my erotic love potion #9 and you're hypnotized... I take you... Just thinking... Knocks on steel doors and I open with a trench coat covering up heavens... No dinner... we skip it but rosè down my panty tine and you don't even know it. I figure I can show it so I sit on your honey like cut brown skin in the dimmest room while I jump on the pole in the living room and ask you if you're ready. Tonight is an adventure and I had to take it slowly. My H-town is on the playlist and *They Like It Slow* is the song. Leg up around the pole as my body constricts it. Lips moving, telling you that this pole is the symbol of your dick and I am now the owner... I have the title to drive. 911 on speed dial... This is a dangerous ride. Slithering up steel poles with no hands... I dropped in splits telling you this is how I'll drop on your dick. Can it do tricks? Can it squirt cocaine shots like magic? Non illusion... No mirage... can you hit it like teenagers in parked cars in a closed garage? Back on the pole I twerk... I learn to put in work. Unbuttoning my coat, I lay it to the side and ask you like Adina, "Do you wanna ride?" Come inside? Fall upon your knees? Can I take you into ecstasy? Will you promise to stay with me? Tricks after tricks and I'm imagining your dick dipped in all my flavors of chocolate. Like a chocolate covered banana... Yes, I lick... I've been thought about it. I can tell what's on your mind but it's just not time.

They had to call an intermission. It was getting hot in there. We resumed fifteen minutes later.

Diamond pumps clicking to redwood floors... I want more and more. I've set up an adventure more like a feast on top of skins. Sushi all over my body and I'm laid on top of tables... chocolate covered fruits embracing my private gates and I tell you to dine till cocaine shots shoot out of this feline and you lick panties till your erection turns to eruptions and I collect cocaine shots on the tip of my tongue and hold it. Adding chocolate to the mixture and I swallow your descendants that will never see earth. Thinking about cocaine shots like a narrow volcano that's been sitting on ecstasy and ready to ignite sweet cocaine shots on my tenants. You slowly dine. Your tongue like chopsticks licking sushi with wasabi sauce off of my inner thighs and I grip the table saying, "I ain't able to wait to taste cocaine as I lick it from your navel". Apple juices and chocolate stains... Migraines from champagne... We toast to the finish of the first course, first round. Your feenin' to go downtown and I'm not ready. Let's go steady. Let's put on old school jams like Luther and Freddy. Maybe a little Teddy... I lie back in a heap of ecstasy and I want you next to me. Let's go steady until the cocaine shots are ready. Again, I ask you like Adina, "Do you wanna ride?" Can you put your legs to the sky? Can you get as cocaine high as I? Are you just mesmerized by the honey in my eyes? You lick honey falling like tears and we reminisce over separated years. I make cocaine shots in your boxers and make all three wishes the same. It would rain between your thighs and in your head rolls your eyes. Slowly, you bite your tongue and say, "Yes, I wanna ride!" See I don't want you to panic. I bought a mechanic for this bull to jump on like Ginuwine in *Pony* and I'd ask you to jump on it and lay on your back while I kiss your sack. Tell you, more like ask you like Adina, "Do you wanna ride?" You'll moan "Yes, ride me tonight!" I'll say gladly with my eyes and ask the mechanic to crank up the ride as I sit securely on your pelvis with your lightening covered by my tornado. I certainly apply that it's a green light and yes, hell yes! Damn baby, let's ride! First speed is too slow. Crank it up! Let's ride! Let my tornado grip your lightening as it gets stronger inside. A deep ride and your dizzy… We're moving like the pacific… More like parting the Red Sea… Rosè dissolved in my tornado… blacking out in ecstasy… you're laying under me. I'm sitting on your pelvis on a mechanical bull dropping cocaine shots out of hurricanes as my tornado covers your lightening. Your lightening gets stronger. You ask me how much? How much longer will I ride? With the mechanic turning the dial and in your head rolled your brown eyes while you dripped waterfalls from your tear ducts happily complying. Shooting off cocaine shots… one after the other… Taking shots to the head like drinking poison after each other. Like dumb Romeo and Juliet or at least Romeo I say. Are you ready for the next round? Do you still want to play? Slowly easing off your lightening rod… Uncovering so much light… Easing off that mechanical bull saying it's just ten o'clock at night. You waddle off the mechanical bull, stumbling and weak. I'd think you were high off cocaine shots. Blacking out from ecstasy and we both rest on the floor while you're lying next to me. I breathe and you breathe and we synchronize heartbeats.

We took our last intermission. That was another fifteen minutes. More people were sneaking off to the bathroom to get busy. Some were heading to the bar to drink the courage they needed to approach the one they liked.

Diamond heels to redwood floors… I sashay to the bathroom 'cause sweating on bulls made me salty. Weak in the knees, you're temporarily mute. No words to speak… No sounds come out so you gesture with your hands. I put my hands on your temporary form of communication and we start to converse. Walking up short stairwells… diamond heels to redwood… Thinking, the adventure is just now starting. Where's the first aid kit? The works... Maybe a defibrillator for his heart because it may stop within the night... The adventure is just now starting. I wonder can he hang with me tonight. Hot showers fogging up mirrors... We step in to save the bill. Rubbing soap of natural oils in the pores of our skin and we slowly wash each other till he grabs me from the back. Wet curls on shower walls... Why he gotta act?! Long showers... Scratching walls... Hair pulling from the back... hand constricting my throat... He asked, "Do you like it like that?" Not knowing payback's a mother... I'm the master of the night! Acting like he was superior and boy he hit it right. Like dunking in the all stars... balls going through the net... Just because wet curls was on shower walls, this event he was going to regret. Letting water slide off the backs of our spines, I whispered in his ear "Do you wanna ride?" it's time and you're mine! I eased him on silk sheets, and put my knees between his thighs. Thought that I should spank him for that last stunt he pulled behind my eyes. I wanted to kiss him slowly. Turn on your back I say! Pressed strawberry juices down his spine and I kiss every juice that's flowing. Nothing would be better so I crawled, diamond heels to silk sheets. I crawl closer to his head, nibble on his ears, kisses to his neck, licks down his spine and bites on his ass. Kissing down his legs, letting no juices pass. Turn over to the front! Pulling out paint brushes dipped in chocolate tracing circles like aliens in corn fields down your chest. I slowly suck chocolate stains off your nipples. Repeatedly looking up at you and I crawl down your body and kiss chocolate stains between your thighs smelling the volcanic heat of cocaine shots as the timer winds down for rockets to shoot off and catch them down my passage then put back into my kingdom. I ride you like a horseman. That knight defending the palace and you squirm while I spank you handcuffed to headboards. Softly biting necks like vampires and I'm in dire need to switch my attire. You erupt your volcanic cocaine shots and I grip it with my palace. Stuck in an unknown wonderland like Alice, you look puzzled and unaware that I rocked your soul out of there. Just a body with no gateway... The eyes are no longer windows. I ease off of your temple and I stare out the window and look back at you sleep. I'm feenin' for you like you were feenin' for me. Now six a.m. and I can't believe we were for so long high off ecstasy. You were sleep next to me and I wanted to give you a present. Like a piece of heaven so I waited till seven, slid my hand between your thighs, as warm under silk sheets, and took you. You were and you only to be with me! I made you breakfast with the works and slid back under sheets... head between your thighs getting cocaine high then I fed you breakfast. I turned over and let you watch me in tune with REM sleep thinking of that ecstasy and how great it was for the adventure taking cocaine shots of ecstasy. While you're laid up next to me, I'm just dreaming as you lean over and kiss me saying, "Thank you for the adventure". You finish breakfast and cuddle next to me as we both dream of that time... so recently ... so high off cocaine shots of ecstasy...

It was too hot and steamy in that room. Everyone was either drunk or tipsy. I had to push Daniel away from me when he tried to lean in with the kissy face. David drove us back to the house and we slept it off. Well they slept. I just stayed awake making sure Daniel didn't try anything while he was drunk. We woke up the next day to the bright sunrise bearing down on our faces. We rushed like Kevin's family on Home Alone. We had to be back home to perform there. I had to finish up my monologue for the audition. We got home shortly after midnight because someone (Daniel) just had to panic on the plane having us thrown out. It was just a little turbulence. We had to catch a new flight that had a two hour delay. I arrived at my house. Opening my bedroom door, I saw Ty sleeping peacefully. I took a shower and brushed my teeth. Next thing I knew Ty was up and so was his "friend". He kissed me. I kissed back. Our tongues was the sweet fulfillment of one another's appetite. He unraveled the towel wrapped around my bare body and picked me up. He sat me on my side of the his and her sink. He started slowly massaging in his two fingers in my yoni, my beehive, my honey pot. My eyes inverted. My pupils got smaller as I looked in his eyes. That look you give when his fingers have damn near shook hands with your soul. He went deeper, in and out, faster with his technique. Yoni was pleased with his patience. She cried out. The antidote for him missing me so. He caressed my breasts one by one. He took turns kissing each one softly. He sucked those nipples till they stood at attention. I was forming a tsunami between my thighs. He picked me up and slammed me down on his master key. We made love on the walls. He put me down and I walked to the pole that I had installed in my bedroom. I lifted myself on that pole and we made synchronized love upside down on that pole. Sixty-nine was the entreé on the menu that we gulped down on that pole without coming up for air. I became Jodie's mother from "Baby Boy". We crawled down off of the pole and headed to the bed. We were still in sync. I was riding that thing up and down as he squatted. Then he laid me down on the bed and pulled out. He kissed my inner thigh and closer to my lower lips. He made figure eights with his licks around my yoni and my clitoris. A triple axle into climaxing and crying tears of joy. He eased himself back inside me. We went from the scizzors, the slingshot, missionary, doggy, spooning. I think we had did about twenty-five positions from the karma sutra book.

"Ooh right there! Don't stop! Faster! Faster! Faster!"
"Damn baby, I can't go that fast"
"Shut up and keep going!"
"Oooh I'm coming!"
"Come baby!"
"Oooooo ... Ahhhh ... Shit! Yes!
"Ooh I'm coming"
"Come inside"

We both climaxed and we rolled over after kissing each other and fell asleep all tangled up. We always slept with some body parts looking like we fell during a game of twister and we landed where our bodies were. In the wee hours of the morning, I woke up screaming out again.

"Sara! Why? Why did you make me choose?"
I cried. Ty woke up.

"It's just a dream. Go back to sleep."

He pulled me in closer to him. As I fell back asleep, he rubbed my back until I was one hundred percent sleep. The next morning I started gathering my thoughts on what I was going to say at my audition. I was nervous and excited all at the same time.

Ch. 35

I also had to start going over the piece I was going to speak tonight as well. We were heading back to Atlanta tomorrow. I had finished a rough draft of my monologue. I kept looking at the letter Sara left me. I just couldn't gather up enough strength to open it. The event tonight was at the cultural arts center on my alma mater campus. It was so big and beautiful. I remember going here to watch plays for credits in college. They were the kind that you'd really just fall asleep on. I made sure that I got that ticket signed by one of the cast for my grade though. Now I walk on campus and see new faces. New teachers walking like they're dog tired already. I walked up the steps and into the area where I was going to be performing at. This hall had the balcony stadium seating as well as the floor seats. One of my old professors introduced me. Dr. Lang was a mix of Vietnamese and Nigerian. He was the most hilarious professor I ever studied under. He was my improvisation professor. I was double majoring in psychology and theatre. He really helped me to get where I am now. I walked to the stage and up the stairs to the mic.

"Thank you for letting me come out tonight and bless the mic. I'm so estactic to be back on campus. I remember Dr. Lang's improv class. He taught me the very bare necessities of performing even if you forget what you've studied. For that I am forever grateful because I improv all the time. Thank you"

He nodded and smiled.

"This piece is called "Too Close"."

Too Close

Friends, friends we got too damn close. We should have remained--... They say once you cross that line you can't go back. I was filling shoes that were not mine. I shouldn't have stayed. Friends, friends we got too damn close. We became lovers. We became crutches for each other. Rebounds for each other... We got addicted to each other. We got too close. Stop! Ahhh! No, don't stop! Keep going! Wait! Bite Me! Shit! I have to go. I can't stay here trying to fill someone else's shoes and losing my identity. We got too close. Let's stay friends. Let's fuck and get it over with. Consumed by lust... I come every time you called. You wanted me and I was bare giving you all of me. We got too close. I'm stopping right now! No, I need you! I need it. How did our friendship turn out this way? How did our love become this painful? Why am I sitting here crying? Crying spells, I rock myself to sleep. We got too damn close. I can't be here. We've totally broken the friendship and can't get away. Can't break away... Trying to pull back but I want you so bad. I want to please you so bad. We got too damn close. I'm suffocating on lust and the crying spells are back. You're sleeping peacefully and I'm here addicted to your dick wondering how did our friendship get to this? Friends, we've now became lovers addicted to each other. Always wanted that last taste of one another... Deeper! Deeper! Shit! Stop! I've got to stop this. Stuck filling someone else's shoes and I still want you. How did it get this bad? Why did we take it so far? I need it. You want me. Addicted to each other... we're each other's kryptonite. We have got to pull away. I want you and you want me. What's good is going to kill us inside. Break away... Break free... Damn... friends, friends we use to be lovers now we don't know each other.

The audience clapped. I bowed. I walked to my car across the street and drove off. I had to head home real fast because I now had to start rehearsing all that I was going to say tomorrow in the audition. Daniel was coming over to help me study. The time came for me to audition. The line was wrapped around the outside and inside of the Phillips Arena. I waited for three hours before they called my name. I walked in the room and I saw Gene Altman and two other judges. One judge was a real sophisticated man with mocha skin and a goatee. The other judge was a tall, fit woman with long curly hair. She looked Hawaiian. I walked on stage to the mic. I was feeling very timid. There were so many emotions going through my head. I blocked out all the negative thoughts and began my audition.

"Why? I tended to ask myself this question daily. If the pain hurt so much then why put others through it? I want to understand why you stayed. I want to feel the reason for accepting your short lived life. I mean I wanted better for you. I wanted us to walk out proud standing in our accomplishments. Why? Why did you stay? What courage lied in that pit to stick it out? What pain seemed so much sweeter to be left unrecognizable countless times over? Why? Why did you stay? I ask myself that everyday? Looking down at your grave and the nightmares never cease. Someone took you from me. Why did you stay? I bled the blood shed tears on my bed waiting for you to call me again. An extended friendship is to it's end. I love you friend. I ask myself this question. I try to find the reasons why. Why did you stay? What was the promise this time? How much did he have to lie to say goodbye? Love doesn't hurt you, people who don't know love does. I'm sitting here looking at this letter you wrote. If I open it, it will be the last part of your voice that I'd ever hear. The last time I'd ever read your slanted handwriting. I'd like to know why you stayed. At least that's what I ask for when I pray. I love you forever and always. Goodbye my love."

I bowed to the judges and exited stage left. I could only hope that they saw the raw emotion when I spoke. I ran to the bathroom, cried, dried my face, and walked out.

Ch. 36

I was still in Atlanta for my show tonight. I needed something to brighten up my day. We still had a lot of time to pass so we went to the Coca-Cola factory and the underground. I just window shopped. My motto is you don't have to spend every time you go out. Just try on clothes for the hell of it. Have fun. Try things that are free for a change. Never think that just because your financial status is one with the elites that you have money to spend just because. Spend but spend wisely so you owe no one. It was getting dark outside. The clouds were setting in for the rain. I don't mind the rain on my natural hair. I danced in it. We headed back to ILounge. I was drained from today but I persevered. I went in that building with a sort of relief. I walked to the mic after a long introduction that really could have been silenced. I grabbed the mic from the host's hands and put it back on the stand and began performing.

"This one is called "The Setup" because some people always tend to have you all the way fucked up."

The Setup

Ugh! Makes me want to scream about how I met you on the scene. Setup by feelings… I was consumed so fast. Played like a violin… Airing out my ass… Shit! Too damn vulnerable! Soft kisses down my neck…. Fingerprints traced down my spine… Felt like eternity when your tongue was crossed with mine. Deep connection I just couldn't control… Setup by emotions… feelings I could no longer hold... Getting deeper in my feelings... Wetter like waterfalls dripping off the ceiling and I'm confused. Pissed off... I want to say I hate you. Damn, double crossed! Setup by emotions... Scratching at old scars... feeling like a fool to have fallen this hard. Don't know what I would say... try not to look your way. I let you open me partially and such sweet kisses betrayed me like Judas. Set up by emotions, I fell deep in a well. Not even burning souls in hell could hear me yell. Pissed at how it was easy. Mad at how good you made me feel. Thought it was going higher... elevator stuck... Set me the fuck up! I guess that was the deal. Got to bury my heart... Ball and chain me to the railroad. Can't be caught catching feelings... Wrecking trains on this emotional rollercoaster... Setup by emotions... Laugh! Cry! Thank you! I can now say I gives no fuck!

You could hear the audience agreeing throughout the performance. Some people were looking at their dates like they wanted to buss some heads. They wanted to fight the knockout round. I kept on with the next one.

"Thank you, this next piece is called "Untrained Hearts". I know we've all been here before. Some of us have been stuck in some hard feelings while the other person has already moved on. Y'all know what I'm talking about.

Untrained Hearts

Leaving untrained hearts... Unsettled... Unaware... Disarrayed... Bleeding there... Beating bare on rare drums... Smoke and mirrors... Still bleeding rose filled tears rewinding to memories over the past decades. Fast forwarding tears to what memories would look like on a feature film over days. Untrained hearts, stuck like a kid between doors on the first day of kindergarten. Learning if he/she should train their hearts to trust another or scream like hell. I yelled inside myself where no one could hear forming ulcers, bleeding out, and counting every last tear. I'm thinking how do you train your heart to stop beating when it's already in the middle of feelings? Stuck like a scratched record. Like an equation on a test that you blanked out on. It's stuck in the middle of his feelings. Your feelings… My feelings keep rehearsing… Aneurisms drilling through my brain, growing on my personality… Feelings on top of soiled skin… I bleed poison and you laugh at me like Quasimodo because I can't seem to hide them. redirect them… untrained hearts, living deep in my feelings as I watch you drift away. My heart keeps beating stuck on feelings. Rather between feelings… between yours and his feelings and another from my past… Although it's long over, unfinished feelings just won't pass. Shit! I'm stick like a prisoner watching a terrorist self suited in c4 knowing life might be over. That bomb will drip tears like crying blood cells of wasted years as it punctures my core and erupts. Disconnected feelings… more like interrupt the center stages of healing and now I'm stuck with unfinished feelings. How do you train your heart to stop beating when it's already in the middle of feelings? Rewind and stop bleeding… Get away and drown it… stop beating… if I could sink it like the titanic and it promises not to panic… No sign of cardiac arrest as it slowly dies in my chest… My mind would be at rest like peace from the hundred years war and over half the soldiers dead. Laid rest for a meaning… coming together through the singing… untrained hearts… How do you train it to stop bleeding when it's shed rivers higher than ceilings? Bleed like crimson baptisms for sinning for being caught up in so many feelings… I was naïve to stop the healing stuck dead center in lust feelings. How do you train your heart to stop beating when it's already in the middle of feelings? Make that bitch choke on cyanide till you make it hard to catch feelings when the oxygen has departed and blood cells are no longer bleeding. Just ask, how do you retrain a heart stuck in the middle of unfinished feelings?

The crowd cheered with "umhmms", "Yes!", and many more head rolling, finger snapping, and duck lip antics. I still kept going to the next one.

"This next piece is called "Love Into Infinity". We all dream of this kind of love. One day I'd like to have it for myself.

Love Into Infinity

To taste the soft touch of your lips… explore the four seasons between your freedom of speech… To enjoy the obsession of your scent… To walk the hallways of your longing childhood… to dine in Eden posing as the illiterate to the rules just to bite the knowledge of your fruit and escape in a world where I now have the freedom to change my environment… To walk the streets of Chicago holding hands without a bullet engraved with my name… to open my first amendment right to cover your fifth amendment protection… To get just enough time in front of a wooden fireplace to brand my signature of affection… to step into a time machine that can let me feel the closeness of your first heartbeat. To be in an anatomical lab just to dissect your frontal cortex and embark on a river down your personality. To strip me down the long walk to freedom and have blood sign my name from your aorta. Feel compressions and hear music as your lungs breathe just to tell your vocal chords to speak to me. Just to see your chest rise and fall like the Berlin wall… To touch your soft ink pen drenched with my DNA signing our Declaration of Independence… To walk on notes harmonious to our synchronized heartbeats rising and falling. I still loved he. Just to do it, I'd do it one last time. Only to mark that I reinvented history, your chemistry, I re-sparked our love into infinity.

Ch. 37

They were still cheering after all that. I told them that this was my last one until the next tour.

"This one is called "If I Had To". I hope you like it.

If I Had To

If I had to remember souls set on fire watching friends and colleagues die at the sins of others. If I had to remember walking on DNA spilled on concrete from someone's innocent little brother. If I had to remember that bullet signed with my name while some faceless sinner ripped out a piece of my heart, putting it in his back pocket, and raping me till scars branded his social security. Remember nightmares and soaked sheets… If I had to remember dying, once for my rights and twice for my freedom being resuscitated into a world where women aren't respected just to keep the fight that I am equal and I deserve to learn. Having the scars to prove I made a difference. If I had to remember the smell of oxygenated blood seeping out cracked backs embedded deep. Feeling heated, sweaty tears falling down my face screaming out for a piece of my heritage ripped out of place and lynched for my burning soul to watch with a numb chord, words I could not say. If I had to remember the desert sands under steel toe combat boots going in a warzone without knowledge of what to expect. Seeing fellow soldiers take their lives and enemies take another. Walking around saying, "What's up" not knowing that would be the last words we ever spoke to each other. If I had to remember watching my kids get ripped out of my arms, executed by terrorist sneaking through my back door knowing all of the years I'll never get to set a memory for. If I had to remember being sold off in foreign lands by the width of my hips and the height of my bones and forced to slave after another man being seen as subhuman. Erased to never know my name... Given the name of my oppressors... Forced to lie with every Tom, Dick, and Harry till I was branded and I could make him what he wanted. Satisfaction... Then they sell of my heart to other sinners teaching them that they are subhuman. I wake up just to name my next set of souls after the first so it's branded, notarized, set in stone who my kids were. If I had to remember waking up to his fist, genes sticking to his knuckles, undoing his belt buckle, and taking it as if I was another man. Just a slave to put him above me and I psychologically keep running back. Keep attaching souls that were never meant to ever know each other. If I had to remember history and all of these cluttered memories archived in my identity, branded into my soul, embedded in my psyche, and knowing that I'd have a responsibility to uphold the justice of my memory. Make every piece of my identity mean something. Let it be that nothing was in vain. I'm not still stuck the same. If I had to remember history where blood done signed my name and bleeding out tears at the thought of every pain, I'd know not to be a fool still sleep, acting like there's nothing left to do.

After I had finished my whole set, I tapped Daniel on the shoulder who was trying to get some girl's number but was failing miserably. I got it for him instead. We walked out and headed back home because we had to head to Los Angeles in three days. My pops was having surgery so I wanted to spend that time with him before I left. I was going to surprise him. You know how women are in my family. They cannot hold water. They can't keep a secret to themselves even if a gun was pointed at their heads. They couldn't even keep a secret if a million dollars was on the line because they're too forgetful to remember which one said not to tell. With that being said, he found out anyway. I got home and checked my voicemail. It was nothing but scammers, mom's reminder of dad's surgery, and Ty asking if I had plans in the coming weeks. I'd call him back later. The next day I had an appointment with David about the permits and all of the hoops that we had to jump through to get them. We still had to find security for the venue. I put on my red and white maxi dress since it was the spring time. I had to leave an hour early to get to 280. Traffic is always the devil when taking this road. I wish we had more scenic routes. You know the back roads that went faster because there were no cops in sight. You could speed as fast as you wanted. Not getting caught was my specialty when it came to driving. I was the ultimate daredevil. I pulled up in the parking deck and scanned my I.D.. This time they were trying to install the new fingerprint sensor to get in the doors of the building. We'll see how far this goes. This new technology is great but they malfunction monthly sometimes a couple of times a month. I got off the elevators and took the stairs. Knocking on the door, I almost witnessed David falling out of his chair through the window.

"Hey"

"Hey David, how's the paperwork for those permits going?"

"Still waiting on a couple of inspections to go, but I should know something by the end of the day."

"That's good. I'm so ready for it to be open already. I've driven by it a few times in awe."

"How did your audition go?"

"It went well I guess. I just want to work with Gene Altman so bad. Just getting that call scares me."

"Why?" He asked.

"I want it so bad and I don't want to get my hopes up."

"You have to keep them up. It's called speaking it into existence. It's called walking by faith and not by sight."

"Yes, I know. I have been speaking a lot of things into existence."

"Where are we on security?"

"I really don't know. I haven't decided which one to use. I'm not about to choose in haste and end up with piss poor service."

"I totally agree. You have to get everything finalized because opening day is creeping up. You need to be ready for the madness."

"I know. I know. I will."

I was about to leave his office when the paperwork came in for me to sign. I signed the paperwork for the licenses and permits. All there was left to do was get security. How hard could it be? I left there and headed back home. Mom had called me earlier and left a voice message reminding me of Pop's surgery. I took I-65S all the way back to the wiregrass. I grew up in the peanut city. A place where it looked like ceramic peanuts were built for every big business there. I rushed to the hospital and waited. I was only staying at home for a day. I decided to take my flight from the airport back home and meet the twins in LA. I didn't want to think on Los Angeles right now. I found my mother and we waited til my Pops had gotten out of surgery. This was going to be the biggest surgery he ever had. It took some hours to get to where they wanted to work on. We were sleep in the room when the phone rang. The doctors had said that his surgery went fine. He was in recovery and we would be reunited shortly. I stayed awake until he came back into the room. Pops took pain like a G. He didn't press the button for morphine that much. I watched his hand the whole time. That's the only way you could tell how bad his pain was. He never made those faces like women do. He always kept a poker face when he was sick. Unless the man told you that he was in really bad pain, you'd never know. Later on that night he fell asleep. I kissed him and told him that I loved him before that. Once he was sleep, I hugged mom and did the same. I went to my parents house, packed my clothes, and drove to the airport. I took my blue luggage to the check-in point and preceded to walk to the waiting area for my plane to arrive.

Ch. 38

I had arrived at LAX and the twins were waiting for me at the gate. I walked through and got in the rental. They started bombarding me with a million questions. It seemed like it.

"Are you excited about the show tonight?" David asked.

"Yes, I am." I replied.

Daniel asked, "Where is your head space with this peace? You think you can get through it without crying?"

"If I do, I'll just pause, regroup, and finish it." I replied.

"Are you still having those nightmares?"

I didn't tell him anything about those. Ty must have opened his big mouth.

"I really don't want to talk about that right now. I just want to go out there and kill it."

"We've come a long way you know." Daniel said.

"It seemed like it all went by so fast." I said.

"I can't believe we hit L.A. status. You're on a different level now." Daniel said.

"You have to step it up. You have performances left and right, movies, auditions, and your new business. Will you be able to handle all of this?" David asked.

"I'm pretty sure I can. Before you all jump the gun, let me just get through this night before y'all start planning my future." I said.

We pulled up at Da Poetry Lounge which is at the Greenway Ct Theatre. I'm excited to see a glimpse of how my future would be in LA. We actually had a scheduled rehearsal. I did the sound check.

I was shocked in myself that I didn't cry during practice. When the crowd started pulling up to the scene I became a little nervous. I felt the rush of performing in one of the biggest cities in the U.S.. What an honor it was to accept their invitation to perform. I was backstage getting my nerves together. I didn't want to be too emotional on stage but I didn't want the audience to feel like I wasn't genuine with my feelings.

"Coming to the stage, an upcoming artist who's known for her powerful pieces. I've been to a few of her shows and you guys would love her. Without further adieu, I give you Ms. Christina Sahará." The Bohemian host said.

"Thank you guys for having me here. Wow, it's so surreal to be performing in LA. I promise to not disappoint you guys. I dedicate this poem to my friend Sara, may she rest in peace."

I felt like I was going to cry so I pinched the bridge of my nose and took a lot of deep breaths.

"My friend Sara was going through an abusive marriage. I've thought many of times what could I have done differently. We were like sisters. I mean we were inseparable. One night turned into the worst night of my life. I had to choose between saving my friend's life or her childrens'. I thought I was making the right decision when I kept our promise to choose her kids. I don't know what I'd do differently if I had that chance. I know in my heart that I at least did something. My friend never made it out of that marriage. I want to tell you all that whatever you are going through. You have a choice to leave. For those of you who have a choice to act on these situations; I beg you to do so. It only takes a village to raise a child, but it takes that same village to stop injustice. Do the right thing!" I said.

I looked out at the crowd and some women were crying. Men were crying. Other women and men walked out. I guess the truth bothered them.

"This piece is called "Domestic Mirrors".

Domestic Mirrors

Bruised on the inside... Looking at my reflection unrecognized, unidentified, trying to give merit as to why I'd ever let him treat me this way. Growing up I'd say, "That would never"... iced words melted... tasting like salt water... bitter like vinegar... I swallow my acidic words mixed with his DNA after his open wounds pound against my soft lips. Broken... I'm looking at my reflection seeing words left unspoken because I died a thousand pieces and I don't know where they are. Shattered like a mirror, don't know how to mend myself to even start. I'm looking at my reflection, salted words, others see at me and like Ariel my voice cannot be heard. Well, why should it be when men get teased with convictions, soft taps on backhands and until the world sees him do it, it turns a blind eye to very hand raised. I'd press charges if it would make a difference but they'd get out and raise another backhand. Fist full of anger, tipsy walking, but my genetic order is drifting in the wind and I'm suppose to know to run. I do... Not dumb... Not stupid... Money talks and nowhere in hell you can go where the devil can't find you. Playing it off like I loved him. Home cooked meals made with wasted DNA from streaming tears I can no longer stop. Won't nothing change until everyone can see his backhand raised... I even showed you my scars fiercely engraved with his DNA and you told me I deserved it being a coward because I stayed. Put your footprints in my soles and walk a mile, maybe a day, look at that reflection that looks like me everyday and tell me who's the coward because I stayed? Until everyone sees his backhand raised, frozen where his flaws are on a platter, forced to eat out of the hand he scarred, don't tell me I'm a coward because I stayed. Looking at my reflection unrecognized, disarrayed, and unnoticeable to myself... See Ray Rice didn't lose it all because his backhand was raised but the world opened broken days watching his fist raised and cold eyes no one wanted to be blamed. They backtracked the delay and shutdown his fame. Not because his hands were raised but because his backhand more like fist rose like stone cold. Get Over Here! Finish her! Half the world makes memes of someone's domestic affairs. Their broken mirrors reflecting unrecognized reflections… Until everyone sees his backhand raised, it's his word against mine! Not a damn thing changed! Laid out on soft pillows covering pain with crooked smiles… Instant replay! Forced entrance into my comfort zone… Spilling his DNA like it never matters. Calling me everything but what I was named… Nope, not a damn thing changed! Until everyone sees his backhand raised and a restraining order is not viewed as just a paper but enforced harder than a drug trafficking sentence. Until they start to take me seriously and know I'm not dumb because I stayed. I stayed because no one's enforcing laws meant to protect me anyway. Hell you've seen that Sandusky case… Hell anything in the world… If closed eyes aren't open and the mindset that protecting my sister is not my business is rehearsed and reinforced. Until everyone sees his backhand raised, no one will notice my urgency for help until I'm six feet under the grave. Faking tears for should've, would've, could haves and not a damn thing changed! Until the world sees him with his backhand raised, yet enforcing the peace, and putting shattered mirrors back together. Don't ask me why I stayed! Closed mouths don't get fed! At least that's when you spoke up when you seen dead bodies overcrowding graves!

I was so happy to finish this piece before I started crying on stage. I literally ran off stage and out the door. I cried then. The twins had walked out after me to see what was going on.

"I know what would make you feel better." Daniel said.

"What?" I replied.

"You got the part." David said.

"What part?" I replied.

"You will now be working with Gene Altman for the next six months in LA. Aren't you excited?" He said.

"You're kidding right?" I asked.

"Nope!" He replied.

I jumped up and down and screamed. I forgot all about the pain and the crying. I get to work with one of black Hollywood's best directors. Before we knew it, I was back home and on my way back to my hometown to see my Pops. I was so excited I started calling everyone. It was the best news I've gotten since that false alarm back when. It was nice to feel accomplished. Everything was lining up for me now. I could see the light.

Ch. 39

I was so excited that I had called my mom to tell her about the good news while I was still on the road.

"Mom, guess what?"

"What?"

"Guess?"

"I'm not in the mood for that. Just tell me."

"I got the part!"

"That's good."

Something was wrong with mom. She would be jumping for joy with news like this.

"Mom, how's it going? What's going on?" I asked.

I could hear her voice trembling as she began to speak. She started crying.

"What are you crying for mom?"

"Your Papa?"

"What about him? What's wrong?"

Her voice made me start crying.

"He's dead. He coded."

"When?" I asked.

"Just a few minutes ago" She replied hysterically.

I screamed. I cried out. I dropped the phone. I was dazed. Within just a few minutes, my world had taken another major hit. He couldn't be dead. I had just seen him and we were laughing about the dumbest of things. I picked the phone back up.

"Mom?"

"I'm here."

"How did he die?"

"They haven't did the autopsy yet. I really don't want them to." She said.

"I'm on my way."

I got there in no time. She had called his side of the family and they were all on their way. I was just in total shock that he was gone. I ran to the room and I could see them cleaning up his bare body. He was lifeless and cold. I ran out of there. Why was this happening to me? Did God hate me this much? Why was I going through all of this? I called Ty and told him. He was on his way. I found my mother and held her tightly. I just felt like I didn't want to lose her either. His family arrived shortly after. Some were very broken up about this. You could see the pain. Some just looked at my mom as if she killed him herself. There was so much that I wanted to say to them but I didn't. I had to be there for my mom and my mother only. When they rolled the body out of the room. My mom screamed and cried out.

"Please, Don't leave me! Don't leave me!"

All I could do was fight the tears. His family grabbed a hold of her and kept telling her to stop making a scene. Making a scene? My mother just lost her husband. She could make hell on earth if she wanted to. They kept telling her that he's gone now and she needed to be an adult about this. I really wanted to go across that face one time. I mean damn! Give her a damn break and let her live! Let her cry it all out. I was trying to be strong while I was around my mom. She needed someone to have the strength for a change. I was so glad to be back at home where I could console my mom alone. My siblings wouldn't be coming in for another day. I just watched my mom the whole time. I guess I was scared. We walked in that house and all of his memories were surrounding us. That night we stayed up late just going over all of the things he used to say. He was the best father God could ever give to raise me. I am grateful for him raising me up to be a respectable woman. My siblings had came in the next day. Honestly, I didn't know what to really say about them. I couldn't explain what I witnessed before they got here. All this death had turned me into a punk. I was just crying all the time for absolutely nothing. It took a while to get everything set. We had to pick out a casket, find the outfit for him to be buried in, plus file for the death certificates. I was with mom every step of the way. He had left her a hefty penny. I was like a pit bull. No one was going to be asking her for any change. This wasn't handout season. This was all that she had left to live off of. Later that week we finalized all the paperwork and places needed for the funeral. I dressed him in his Armani suit that I had just bought him for Christmas. It was a promise that we had. He was rooting for me to get married. I guess I'll never get that chance to be escorted down the aisle. When time came for the funeral, all hell broke loose. Scheduling was off and we were running late. His family had beat us to the place. It was okay because we were going to have a great day. We were going to send off the man that we looked up to with a bang no matter what. I cried out and mom cried out. I hyperventilated. It was just a day I really wanted to get over. We all got to share our favorite memories with our father, the man that raised us. There was not a dry eye in the building. I noticed everyone was here but Jennifer again. I understand her not being there for Sara. This was me. I had been there for everything and her absence was very loud to me. I turned back around and kept looking at the casket sitting in front of me. I cried out.

"Don't leave me! Please, Don't leave me! I have no father now!"

As they finished the memorial service, the paulbearers had carried him out to the grave site. I ran the other way. I could hear my mother screaming as I looked on from afar.

"No! Baby, Don't leave me! I'm coming with you! Please, Don't leave me here! I love you!"

They lowered him in the ground and we walked away. I just couldn't take it anymore. I didn't know why it had to be my life that was being shaken up so hard.

Ch. 40

I had pretty much quit. I wouldn't go anywhere. Brittani called me.

"Hey girl, how are you holding up?"

"Not too good. I'm trying to keep it together."

"How's your mom?"

"How do you think? She has been up all night every night."

"I know it's rough. There's nothing that I could say to ease the pain. I've lost a parent but everyone is different. You will get through this as well."

"After this hit, I really don't want to. I just want to leave this world so that I won't get hurt again."

"Well you can have a pain that hurts like hell but heals eventually. You'll start living after while. You can have the pain that is hell. That pain tortures and torments your soul. That is your choice. I have to go. I'll call you later."

"Okay, bye"

She was right. It would get better but in the now, I just couldn't see it. I don't want to see it. I had the part for a major role. I was soon opening my new poetry cafè. I was going solo on my tours. That didn't matter if I didn't have him cheering me on or making me laugh. What was I suppose to do now? I thought about what that lady said a while back about killing herself. Right now, I would surely be tempted to try it. The phone kept ringing and people kept calling me to check on my well being. Mom was sleep in her room, I didn't want to bother her. We had been through so much. Every time that

I got to myself I started crying. The twins had came to the house to check on me.

I was crying hysterically.

"Hey" Daniel said.

"Hey y'all"

"We came to check on you."

"I'm doing fine."

I was taking shots of everything in my wine cabinet. My mom was staying with me for a couple of days. It was just so she could clear her mind for a while.

"That tone says different." David said.

"Guys, I really just don't want to do this anymore." I said.

"Do what?" David asked.

"Do this. I don't want to be on tour traveling all week. I don't want to do the film or finish with the opening of the club. I just want to be left alone and to this alcohol." I said.

"That isn't good for you when you are in pain. You can't drink your life away because life happened. Shit happens! We can't control the life that we are dealt. We can only make it better by the choices that we choose to make." Daniel said.

"Why should I be the only one choosing?" I yelled.

"It's your life. The only way you are going to get out of this funk is if you choose life and life it freely." David said.

"Say that to all the dead and armed kids." I said.

I knew they meant well but I just didn't want to hear anything but the ugly sound of my voice while I cried. They left. Over the next few days mom was exercising and leaving the house. Mom was doing better than I was. I had to ask her.

"Mom?"

"Yes baby?"

"How do you do it?" I asked.

"Do what?" She replied.

"How do you build the strength to keep moving after you just lost your husband?" I asked.

She replied, "It isn't easy losing someone you love. God was able to show me the true meaning of love. That man loved me with every part of his being. I have my moments. I cry at times but I have to keep living."

"That just seems so hard to do."

I really don't get how she's so strong. She just buried the man of her dreams and she is still living. She is still following her passions. I just laid down on the floor and cried. I couldn't do this. I couldn't play this game. There was literally nothing to live for.

"Get up!"

"For what? I've lost my best friend and the man I looked up to. What the fuc--."

"Language! We're not going there. Get your butt up off this floor! Get up! Get your life together. Finish your dreams like you promised him. You're not about to be laid up on this floor giving up. If I can't give up then you are not about to either."

"Why not? What's the point in all of this?"

"I don't have that answer. You need to go to God for this. I've been through much worse. I've beaten cancer, lost a parent, been through hell and back. Now I have lost my husband and I'm just not going to let this tear me down."

"You're just going to act like he didn't exist?"

She replied, "That's not what I said. I can't give up every time I witness pain. I have to push through it. I cry. I will cry more when I watch movies that he liked, smell cologne that he use to wear, see someone who looks like him, or anything that brings me back to a memory we shared. I have to be okay! I have to get through this! You need to too."

"Yes ma'am" I said while wiping my face with my hands.

She always had the strength that I hoped to have one day. I know she's been through so much. Her strength is out of this world. I decided to finish what I started. If my mom could be strong even when she's weak then so can I. I told my mom that she could stay as long as she wanted to. I didn't want to rush her into going back home. It was just her and him. It does feel weird to walk into a place that you shared with someone for so long and realize that they won't ever be coming back there. I walked upstairs. I ran that shower til the temperature was almost hot. I undressed out of my graphic tee that read "I Will Not Be Less Than..." and my pants. I took of my black laced panties and bra. I stepped into the shower and pulled the glass door back. I stood in there and let the water hit my body. It dripped off like dew on a tree. I just wanted to baptize my thoughts in this shower. I wanted all of this pain to be drowned in this water before I stepped out. I grabbed my dove body wash and lathered up my loufa. I began massaging it into my skin. I rinsed off, pulled the door back and grabbed my bath sheet. I never understood why they called it that. Just say the extra large towel please. I walked out the shower in my towel, brushed my teeth, and walked in the walk-in closet. I grabbed a camisole and some jeggings. I began packing. I looked at my room and knew that I had to wash clothes sooner or later. There was so much going on that I really didn't care to. Tomorrow we were headed back to Miami to the Bohemia Room. I guess I needed to breathe. My dreams gave me life. I'm glad my mom gave me that talk because I couldn't see myself walking away from my dreams this close. I called David and told him that we could go on with the tour. Since my mother and friends weren't going to let me give up, I guess I'd have to push through. I slept for four hours tops. My alarm went off at four in the morning. I gathered my things and went downstairs. Daniel had text me that he was outside. I really didn't want to talk to him. I put my headphones in my ears, turned on my music and fell asleep. We made it to Miami by mid evening. I walked in to the club and headed straight to the bar. I took three shots of whatever was the strongest. I took a deep breath and walked on stage. This was the first time that I would be performing in a month. I just had to get over this hurdle. It always feels awkward to be back working on your dreams when your support system starts breaking down.

"Thank you all for being here in support. I apologize for the wait. I hope you like what I have been working on."

I closed my eyes and tried not to cry. I didn't. I began my first piece.

"This is called "Too Different Thoughts"." Sometimes you get mixed signals. You step back, adjust your own feelings to the situation, and move on.

Too Different Thoughts

Long conversations… Years apart… Distant lovers… Ripped hearts… Reconnected and our souls are more like disconnected. Proton falling for a neutron, we cancel each other out. Different… I'm needing a given blessing. You're saying soft caressing. I'm thinking perfection. You're thinking fucking. I want marriage. You want a cunninlinguist connection. A fellatio type of expression… A mind erasing seduction that gives you selective amnesia and a free wheelchair ride… Damn! I'm nervous to see you. Your intentions are already panned out. Mind shutdown like the system… Regurgitating ejaculated generations… Unwanted nations… Shit! Deeper than I wanted! Not wanting to be another pussy pulsating situationship … An asexual relationship… A one sided emotional rollercoaster… That inevitable friendship where I demand the dictatorship… More like dominatrix, the master of your 8-9 inch ship. Doing it to myself… Over thinking… Planning too far ahead… Too different levels of the same game… Doing it to myself… Shit! I should have never met you! Friendships were easier before walls constricted pythons. Feelings turned to cast iron, pot bellied ovens spitting out the pits of hell fires. There's nothing left from you to desire.

The crowd clapped.

Ch. 41

I went on to the next piece.

"This last piece is called "Jeza-Jezabel". Hope you enjoy it."

Jeza-Jezabel

Don't look me in the eyes. You see, in my eyes, staring weakened generations you haven't begun to make. Nations you haven't even birthed… You see, in my eyes, staring is like wildfires in deep forests setting head to every muscle in your body. You see, in my eyes, staring causes to shake at the thought of my soul touching it. Rivers to dry out from my tongue caressing it… A come hither crawl… Aphrodite rises on the other side of the sun. My fire suffocates like a mating anaconda swallowing you whole after she comes, climaxes, finished with whatever man you thought you were. Don't look me in the eyes! You see, in my eyes, staring slays every thought you ever had of correct paths. I venture out and explore your core. The finer make of a man… Your anatomical position… Bull riding that's never failed… Don't look me in the eyes, please! See staring… See staring… See staring causes friction. The English dick-tionary supplies more words than the world has time. I ask you please don't look me in the eyes. I have slain every generational descendant you ever had before conception. I've weakened nations before you ever had time to build morals, experience, memories I've killed. Stop! Just don't! Please don't look me in the eyes! A foresight you can't stand to resist. Dropped stares… Looks turned to touch… Touch to souls intertwining… Consummation to fallen kingdoms… Stop! I tried to warn you.

The crowd cheered. Mostly the women. Some were snapping their fingers. Women giving their men those awkward looks. I loved Miami. It was one of the cities where I was pretty much promised diversity. Diversity was beautiful in its own right. There were so many Latin Americans, Islanders, and Africans. It was a beautiful sight to see. I missed my girls being around me. I missed our talks. I invited them out to dinner when I got back home. They were all in places where they couldn't just take a vacation. I thought that I would bring the mini vacay to them. We had been to too many funerals as it is. When I got back home. I ran upstairs to my bed and kissed my sheets. It was so good to be back in my bed. It was good to go to hotels but nothing is like being in your own bed. I never had to worry about whose nasty ass had their secret rendezvous in the bed I was sleeping on. I definitely didn't have to worry about what STI'S I may have contracted by sleeping on this bed. My cousins would bring their own sheet sets to the hotel. They would replace the items with their personal ones until checkout then they would put the spread provided by the hotel back on the bed and leave. I put my things down and rested for a while. I knew that I would eventually have to get up and meet my friends at Papadeaux. We all had to be dressed up. They picked the restaurant. I went along with it. I picked a nice sky blue sundress. I had my white Louis Vuitton pumps on. I wanted to wear the hat. I just took my hair out of it's twists, picked out my roots with my black pride fist pick, and shook my hair. I sprayed on my Versace perfume. I had the perfume for most of my college life and I still have that bottle. I guess I just didn't want to use it up too quickly. I got in my car and drove to the restaurant. We were seated fast. Brittani had on her favorite dress, the black dress with the back out. Natalie had on a red sundress with pearls. She kept them pearls on for dear life. She was apart of Alpha Kappa Alpha sorority. She wouldn't go a day without her pearls. She says they make her day better. We ordered red wine for the table.

"I've missed you guys so much." I said.

"I've missed y'all too. It isn't the same without my girls." Britt said.

"It really isn't. Life seems bland without y'all. Our friendship is like salt to our day." Natalie said.

"Where's Jennifer?" I asked.

"She isn't coming. I've tried calling her multiple times and she hasn't answered." Natalie said.

"We all know that girl really didn't want to be around us. She just wanted perks. I don't know why y'all expect her to show up anywhere. She flakes under pressure." Britt said.

"This isn't pressure though. We're just having a girls day out and catching up on each other's lives." I said.

"I'll try again." Natalie said.

"Don't bother. She wasn't there when Sara died or when Tina lost her dad." Britt said.

"Yeah, I could understand her not being there for Sara's funeral. I knew she didn't care much about her. I would have thought that she would be there for me. I've been there for her through so much shit." I said.

"You remember the miscarriage, the constant crying, the abuse, jail, and the rehab. I just don't get how a person could not be there for someone who has been there so much for them." Britt said.

"It's whatever. I don't even care anymore. I just got the keys to the club."

"OMG, I'm happy for you." Natalie said.

"Congrats Tina. How does it feel to be close to your dreams?" Britt said.

"It feels good but scary at the same time. I dreamed about this. I never dreamed about all of the pain I had to go through to get to it." I said.

"Sometimes we have to experience the worst nightmares of our life, face out fears, or go through the hardest of pains to get to the sweetest part of life. Sometimes the people we love don't make it out to see those dreams come true. We have to push through then pay it forward for them." Natalie said.

"All I want to know is can I get free drinks when you open it? Britt asked.

"Um, I might have to limit your drink intake. You like to strip when you're drunk. I can't have that. I need to keep the business open not have it shutdown before it even gains success." I stated.

We all laughed.

"I already see you as successful. We all are successful. I'm graduating with my doctorate in Neuro this May. You're about to open up the club and already on a sucessful tour. Natalie is about to graduate from nurse practitioner school in May as well. We are all successful." Britt stated.

"Yes, We are." I replied.

Our food arrived and we ate. When we had came to the dessert part, my plate had a Tiffany jewelry box on it. I looked around like which psycho trying to ask me to marry him. I've been proposed to by the weirdest people at the most inconvenient times. The girls were smiling hard. I heard "Will You Be Mine" by Ruff Endz playing on the speakers. Ty had on this black and gold pinstriped suit walking around the corner of the restaurant. I looked at the girls. They kept this from me. Ty grabbed my hand and got down on one knee.

"Christina, we have been through so much together. I have loved you for some time. I knew you were the one for me a long time ago. I know you have been through the worst these last couple of months. I want to be by your side and love you as your husband. If you'd have me, I'd like to make this official. Will you, Christina Sahará Rhodes, be by wife?"

I cried. I was speechless in that moment. The man of my dreams had proposed. All I could think of was that I wouldn't have gotten to this part had I have given up and took my life. Then my thoughts had fast-forwarded to my future and I began crying again. I had realized that no one would be walking me down the aisle. My stomach tightened.

"Yes, Yes I will marry you."

He stood up and we kissed. My friends were crying and so were the other people in the restaurant. Everyone clapped. My friends were wiping the tears from their eyes with their napkins. It was the happiest moment in my life after all that pain. I knew that I had to keep on fighting to see what else life had to surprise me with. Ty had wiped the tears from my face. My friends started taking pictures of myself and the ring. The ring was a four carat black diamond ring with canary diamonds around the band. It was the prettiest thing I've ever seen.

"I'm going to take this picture so I can post it. This is my ring for just a moment." Britt said.

"Girl, you're not touching my ring now. I don't see why you have to post that anyway." I said.

"I have to make it seem like I'm unavailable." She replied.

"Competing with that man is stupid. You know if he sees that ring, you might have to pay child support." Natalie said.

Britt replied, "Pshh, like hell I will! I will not now nor will I ever pay that man a dime in child support."

"How's the kids? I asked."

Ty had already pulled up a seat. I guess he was going to join in the conversation as well. He just listened.

"They're fine. This fool wants them to visit him for the summer."

"That's not a bad idea." Natalie said.

"Girl hush, he might be the father but I swear he's never around. I wonder if I send those bear cams with Jace and Brandon would he notice?" Britt said.

"Brittani, Don't do that. It's their dad." I said.

"Y'all don't know him like I do. I worry when they are out of my sight. I have two sons. I don't want anything to happen to them. I know he'd be too busy with work to attend to them. I don't want them being one of those latchkey kids. I just have a gut feeling that this is not what I need to do." Britt said.

"Okay, ultimately it's your decision." I said.

"Yeah, we can only give you advice." Natalie said.

We finished dessert and we went deutch. I met Ty at my place.

Ch. 42

We had came back to my place all excited. I was so happy to be Tyler's fianceé. It felt good saying that. I kept looking down at my ring in awe. I couldn't believe this was actually happening. I wanted to thank him for being there for me through all of this. I went upstairs and I dressed into something sensual. I showered up and put on this satin red lingerie set. I gave a little leg action through the door like Eartha Kitt in Boomerang. I pointed at him from the room and called out his name. I motioned for him to come into the room. He walked up the stairs already undressing. When he came in the room, he had nothing on but his pants. I pushed him on the bed. I had put on my "Quiet Storm" playlist. It was a mixture of Babyface, Keith Sweat, Adina Howard, 112, Jodeci, Silk, H-town, and Luther Vandross plus many more. The first song was "Nasty Grind" by Adina Howard. I started wining my hips slowly. I climbed up on that pole and landed in a split. I eased up then stood up. I started wining in Ty's lap. He was rock solid already. The playlist kept playing song after song. I grabbed his master key. I unlocked my own fortress within my yoni. Sweet juices flowed between the both of us. We made love kissing each other. He pulled my hair and started sucking my neck. Sucking like he was a vampire on the hunt for blood. I rolled my eyes back and bit my bottom lip. He went so deep inside. He might as well have written a love letter on my female counterparts. I didn't want it to end. He had that steady rhythm. I didn't want to interrupt that. It was pleasant. We climaxed at the same time and we fell asleep. Well he did at least. I just sat up in bed and looked around the room.

It just doesn't feel real that I'm engaged and everything is lining up for me. My eyes started getting heavy and my thoughts fell asleep. I had to get some kind of rest because I was going back on the road tomorrow. We were heading back to Jackson, Mississippi. I promise I was getting tired quickly lately. I really wanted at least a week off but that wasn't happening. I asked for this. I wanted my life to speed up. I just never thought it would be this fast. The next morning I woke up with breakfast sitting beside me with a note from Ty saying he's heading home and that he'd be back later. Those homemade biscuits, sausage links, three eggs scrambled with cheese, and Belgium waffles were to die for. He was trying to thicken me up. I finished my breakfast and got dressed. I had to pack early because I never knew when something was going to happen. Nowadays I had to be ready for whatever came up. Daniel picked me up by himself today. I really didn't speak to him like that anymore. I really wanted to fire him but him and his brother were a packaged deal. I just used them as eye candy. We got to the club at about nine at night. I walked out in my blue jumper and blue suede shoes. The crowd was waitin on me anyway. I approached the mic and began my show.

"Hey, thank you all for coming. I want to thank you for bringing me here again. This piece is called "I Am Sara". It's more of a historical piece of work. It's not something I do often. I hope you enjoy it." I said.

I Am Sara!

Sara, from my roots they called me. Saartjie, as I servant I was named. Only history remembers me as Venus, the "Hottentot Goddess". Tricked into exploitation… Swept under contracts of servitude… exploited against rights… I'd travel across Europe in a cage half naked. Gees, now they tell me in your world that they do it freely… Praising the glory of everyone seeing assets not meant to be seen in public… No decency to ever be a woman… You are now an object! A display caged where men fantasize over disruptive fantasies. Where young girls put bodies in the hands of snakes to be just like this object, self exploiting, something I did not understand. You are now an object! The new "Venus"… I'm here watching, illiterate to know not even a word they said and you're happy bouncing it up and down in a cage. Strip life… Forced to not have an identity… Pushed away from my own heritage… brutally fucked, legs spread wide open… Took every serpent into my bosom and gazed at the sky. Crying, why me? It's money to you. It's your right, you say. Well will you thing of me, one without a say, opened legs for the world to see? Every Tom, Dick, and Harry free to slither and spray up in me… Your ass… Your ass… your assets should be covered! Sara… Saartjie… Venus… Who am I now? Naked, barely half, body glorified amongst crowds and yet you will squat for the world to see asses. Like balancing champagne glasses on fake asses is talent?! Damn! The world's so twisted and I'm glad I'm not in it. What is this twerking that you do? Just sit it all down all of you! Listen to the masses instead of showing off your asses making exploitation a trend. Money means nothing when the snake has your soul. See it swaying side to side. The minute you lose your gaze, the cobra will strike. Sara… Venus… Which one am I? An unidentified body traded and forced to take commands like an animal. I'm caged and studied by scientists. My anatomical body being visually dissected just to emphasize that my culture, my race was lesser and oversexed. Oversexed? Nothing compares to what I see in your world. Too eager and freely drop dresses, let down tresses, spread it wide and drill it deep. While mothers weep at their knees wondering how this could ever be. Sara… Venus… Who am I? Losing identity, I'm in an identical cage to an animal as big as me. Exploited to look ridiculous and you celebrate exploitation! You live for the money. Die and money will still be here without you. God was here before me and it sure as hell is here now. Like fish, you fall for the same bait. Born into the same trait… Going on the same date… Money will be on the same plate but your morals won't. Lying to myself about living conditions… Now I'm dead… My soul is watching my body apart, dissected and stuffed for the world to see. My pickled pussy in jars for the world to get a close up… I am human! I am a woman!

Still stuck on my body you see… Sara… Saartjie… Venus… Which one is me? Lost my identity trying to reclaim my soul… Looking at your generation, self esteem too grounded in holes suffocating on toxic called media. Where is your reality? Sara… Venus… Servant… Slave… I am just Sara, I Say! It's your turn. You are just an object! The new age Venus! Self caging… Self exploiting… Self esteem is in vomit filled toilets. I am Sara! You are now the slave! Self chaining to the system… Sadistic as it sounds, you like the cracked backs of whips as you don't give a fuck… Doesn't matter… To the new age Venus, a toast to self hatred! I am Sara! My soul, just save it! I am Sara! You can have Venus!

Everyone clapped. I bowed. We all walked out. I didn't want to stay longer. I had to get back. David noticed the ring.

"I see he took the first step to commitment."

I looked down at my ring.

"Yes, he did." I replied.

"You're getting engaged? Congratulations! Daniel said sarcastically.

"Don't mind him, he's just mad because he never said it first." David said.

"I'm not mad at all." I replied.

We arrived back in Birmingham. We took 65 back to my house and took exit 259. When we pulled up to my house, I switched my shoes to something more comfortable. There's nothing worse than walking in shoes that you haven't patiently broken in. I unlocked my door and walked in. I checked my messages. It was the same old thing. Bill collectors wanting money, credit scammers trying to steal money, and mom with the lecturing. I decided to call my mother back before it ever got hostile.

"Hey mom"

"Hey, what's this I hear of you getting married to this boy?" She asked.

"Who told you?" I asked.

"I have my eyes and ears out there. Don't act like I can't find out about any of my children." She replied.

"Yes, I am getting married. Ty proposed."

"About time that man did something good." She said.

"He always does things for me. You just don't hear about it." I replied.

I began crying.

"What you cring for? I thought this was what you wanted."

"I do want it."

"Then why are you crying?"

"I have no one to walk me down the aisle. I will be taking the road by myself."

"You never have to go it alone. God is always there."

I tuned her out at this point.

"I know"

"Things will work out for you? I have faith that they will."

"I know"

"Is that all you have in your vocabulary?" She asked.

"No ma'am. I have to go though. I'll talk to you later. I love you. Bye!"

"Love you too. Bye!"

All of these deaths have been hitting me back to back. It's hard knowing what you dreamed of isn't exactly how it's going to come out. I guess I'll just have to fold and pray like my mama says. I will not give up being this close to success.

Ch. 43

Today was a more emotional day for me. It certainly was not one of my good days. I looked at that envelope that Sara had left for me cherishing whatever words she had on those pages. I didn't want to open it yet. I didn't want her last thoughts to be read just yet. The tears fell down my face. I took deep breaths and wiped them away. I had to start packing for Tampa. Most of my wardrobe were swimsuits. I planned on heading to the beach. David drove this time. I rolled down the window and let my curls fly in the wind. Normally I wouldn't do this because I was trying to preserve my hairstyle. This time I let my mane have its freedom. Halfway point I fell asleep. I was already nodding off. I would wake up as if someone was calling my name then fall right back asleep. We arrived there mid day. We tried not to stop as much. We both made a pact to not have anything that would send us to the bathroom. I guess it worked. When we got there we found the closest restaurant and went strictly to the restroom. Even though we could afford what was on the menu, we weren't going to spend that much money on a meal. We found the closest Wal-Mart and stocked up on food. We arrived at the venue thirty minutes early to rehearse. Once the crowd started packing out the place, we began taking our places at the club. The host introduced me and I took the stage.

"What's up Tampa! It's so good to be back in the sunshine state. This piece is called "50 First Dates". This took me to a place I don't ever want to return again. I hope you all enjoy it though."

50 First Dates

The moment you feel you're just living going on fifty first dates of the same comatose reality... Doing the same paralytic movements... Just nothing... Just existing... Just living just to breathe... Those same 50 first dates of self in a mirror looking back at you... Life doing 180s... You're in quicksand filled holes trying to dig out memories of where it all fell. Where life just stood still... Why you can't grasp the fact that your world is changing and you're stuck on the same 50 first dates. Sheltered for protection... Body's changing... Life is changing and it's been Sunday for the past three years. Can't even enjoy the change because you no longer have the knowledge to... Waking up to a video of the future because your mind can't process any further than that Sunday when your world went into paralysis. When your brain stopped processing a clean slate... When your heart couldn't get over that Sunday so it stayed there... it wouldn't even beat for the present having been paused for the past. 50 first dates of the same thing for normalcy... 50 first dates of the same kind of relationship... Stuck on the same drama... 50 first New Year's resolutions of the same ignorance you just brought the New Year in with... 50 first dates of complacency... It's funny because I've been on 50 damn first dates in three years and can't seem to reach the change. 50 first dates of sulking in "What ifs"... 50 first dates of dramatic crying as to why I'm stuck here... 50 damn first dates of the same paralytic expressions... Where the hell am I going?! 50 first dates... Too many gifts hidden in mines of my being... 50 first dates of only me knowing what the fuck I'm doing... 50 first dates of loneliness... Paralytic dysfunction... 50 first dates, a film I cannot stop from skipping because 50 first dates happens to be my paralytic life.

They clapped. They cried. I bowed. I cried. I wiped my tears away with the back of my hand and walked off stage. I had to rush everything lately. I had to head out to Cali for the first shoot of the film. I also had a performance at the Bakery Poetry Lounge. I had enough packed so I didn't have to go home. David drove back to Birmingham and I flew out to California. It was a place for endless possibilities. I arrived at LAX and my driver was already waiting for me. He took my bags and we headed for the car. We arrived at the studio within three hours. I was like a kid in the candy store. I had to keep my composure because I was not a child and this wasn't the candy store. It was such an honor to actually be on set with Gene Altman. They showed me to my trailer with all of my outfits for my scenes. I slammed the door and screamed. This was really happening. I was really about to be directed under the most powerful female director ever. I changed clothes and walked back on set. My first thing was sitting at a bar to lure in the man that would soon be my husband.

"Action!"

I began walking to the bar. I sat down on the chair and turned towards the door with my legs crossed. It had to show my leg through the split.

"Christina, turn your head left. Chin up! Stick out your chest! Shoulders down!" She ordered.

It looked like I was in pageantry 101. It was so many nonverbal communications in this scene that I couldn't wait to fast forard to the good part.

"Christina, when he walks up to you I want you to smile then drop your head."

I followed orders. Okay, I knew this part. This part is when I lifted up my leg and slid it down his chest and circled it around his manhood. There were so many angles that they had to shoot it that my leg was getting tired. It was still exciting but I was too tired. We all ended that day for that scene. I was just happy to get it over with. I had to rush out of here and back to my hotel. I had to get ready for my performance as well. I had too much on my plate but I needed it. A booked schedule was my way of coping through the pain. I didn't have to face it that much. I didn't want to face it at all. I cried at night all the time. I walked back to my trailer to change. I had two missed calls from Brittani. I called her back to see what was going on.

"Hey Britt Bratt, what's up?" I asked.

"Jace is dead!"

Everything happens in threes they say. Death happened like a huricane to me just picking up my life and tossing it around. I felt numb at this point. I felt like the wicked witch on The Wiz. Please don't bring me no bad news! Get over one trauma and you think you're free then you get hit with an even bigger trauma, then another one. I guess life doesn't care who you are as long as it can shit on you.

"What?! How?" I asked.

"It was his spring break and I sent him to his dad's for a trial run. I thought that he would be okay. I thought that he would be safe. I should have went with my gut. I should have never trusted that man with my child." She said. She started crying even more.

"How did he die?" I asked.

"He had walked over to a friend's house down the street. He was walking back home when a cop stopped him. He had his music playing in his headphones so he didn't hear anyone. They told me they thought he had a gun when he reached down in his pocket but all he had was his cell phone because his dad was calling him." She explained.

I started crying. My godchild is now dead. This could have been avoided. He was only twelve. They didn't have to shoot him.

"The worst part of it all is that they fired fifty rounds in the back of my son. They had on the report that they feared for their lives and he was charging at him. My scrawny twelve year old son charging at them. Really?!"

I was speechless. I didn't know what to say about this. What was there left to say? Words weren't going to bring him back. The only thing left was to act upon such things so that no one else has to go through this. I watched all of these cases on television. I never knew pain until it hit close to home. It was a snotty nosed kid that I use to babysit. A kid I helped potty train. It was a kid that I tutored. He was very talented. He loved science all too well. They murdered our future and lied about it being their fault. I was sick to my stomach. I opened the door to my trailer and text my driver that I was ready to be picked up. I was still on the phone with Brittani. I don't know a mother's pain but I'm damn sure close enough to feel it.

"I'm in California right now. I could call David and see if he would take the case."

"I-I-I just want my son back. I want to hear his sweet voice again and tell him that I love him. I want to tell him congratulations on his good grades. I won't be able to do any of that. They took him from me!" She screamed.

"I'll be home shortly. Just be strong you hear me." I said.

"I hear you!" She said.

I didn't know what else to do. Shortly after, we hung up. I had to begin praying. My soul was empty but I felt like I needed to do something to help out. I had to give the last of what I had.

Ch. 44

Trying to wrap my mind around what Brittani just told me was painful. I wrote this piece not knowing that it was going to hit this close to home. I arrived at the lounge and went straight to the bar. I had to drown this pain the best way I knew how. I know alcohol wasn't the way to get through the pain. In this moment, it was the serum to get me through this performance. I walked on stage and began crying already.

"I'm sorry guys. Please bear with me. I just lost my godbaby to a senseless act of violence. He was twelve and gunned down by the police. His future was ripped away from him. Could you imagine burying your own child after you've gotten to know him? Excuse me."

I took a minute to gather myself. I wiped away the tears with the tissue the host gave me.

"Sorry for that. This piece is dedicated to my baby. It's called "Tagged". I hope you love it.

Tagged

Tagged! Faces dried up in body bags… slaughtered innocence on badges… Memories choked on like swallowed ashes and I see eyes, eyes of those who futures were decided by one's discrimination. Their racial hatred… Don't get me twisted, it ain't always a smoky mirror… A duped mirage… A clouded CO_2 filled garage… Pictures… Names… Sound off! Sean Bell! Oscar Grant! Mike Brown! Ezell Ford! John Crawford III! Victor White III! Tamir Rice! Eric Garner!

Countless others tagged, dried up in body bags and they tell me to know my rights. Sound off! I have the right to refuse consent of searches of myself, car and home! I have the right to film/record traffic stops! I have a right to decline police questions! I have the right to request and record officer information! I'll give you my license and registration as a means of cooperation. Don't get it twisted, I have a right to leave if not under arrest! Am I free to go yet? Yet I listen as no one remembers that day in history class where testing on your rights would mean choosing death or life. Homeruns or strikeouts… Still I see my people tagged, dried up in body bags, or slavery called the prison system. Incorrect grammar in 3-2--, "We ain't on a chain gang no mo!" Tax paid prison systems… No wonder the lost want to go back… State of the art, they say… Can't beat that! Tagged, my mind dried up in body bags. A mind that doesn't know its rights can't set itself free from a lie. If I had to dip back in history, I'd take a look at the Bill of Rights versus me. I have rights! I have the right to free speech, press, and assembly. Why does it come at a price? A march seems like a death warrant signed in blood. I have a right to bear arms. Number four, no unreasonable search and seizures, no criminal prosecution and punishment without due process, and a speedy trial by a jury of my peers. Why does this jury look twenty seniors from my years? Too old for my age… Too biased on race and they all save face because eighty percent is of no race of mine. Maybe one, just one percent looks like me. My right prohibits excessive bail, excessive fines, and cruel and unusual punishment. Is killing off races not unusual to you? Oh yeah, blood was signed when Native Americans were slain. Tagged, rights zipped up in body bags. One sided stories… Tell me how your white lie cost them their future? Live on the day you slain them before they were even shot. Tamir Rice, tagged! History is slept on, bought in slain bodies dried up in bags. Thirteenth amendment abolished slavery. Tell me why I feel like a slave in my own country? Fourteenth said all who were born in the U.S. were citizens in where they reside. The fifthteenth said all citizens should not be denied the right to vote by race, color, or condition of servitude. It didn't apply to m until 1965. Voting rights, title II of the Civil Rights Act of 1964 prohibited discrimination in certain places of public accommodations. That doesn't mean I can't get tagged. Cold words cutting through big hearts, death stares, followed like I can't pay for what I want. Acting like I don't see them cleaning merchandise because they see a leper and not a human… I'm tagging myself if I take offense to ignorance and not rising past mountains of what they paint me to be. Tell me why Brown vs. Board of Education invalidated racial segregation in schools yet 360 degrees and it seems like we have to fight to sustain it? In our minds, oh in our minds, we are separate anyway teaching different ways to survive, teaching our children that we too have history, inventors, and peace prize winners rich in foundation. We don't have to be tagged dropped off in body bags, print less, fingers unidentified yet you're wondering how it all ties in. Yet again, a mind that doesn't know its rights can't free itself from a lie. Target… Not useless… More like priceless… Indefinite sense of self knowing where I came from and how I'll arrive… Ambition and drive… Tagged! See we've gotten ourselves entangled with the mindset of being nameless in body bags and foregoing rights to keep them from talking. Where are we walking? On the hotter side of hell… Dumb enough to not know how to save ourselves… I've said this two times before, a mind that does not know its rights can't free itself from a lie. Now you're left tagged and swept up in body bags. The world only remembers you on your birthday and the anniversary of your death. Tagged! Unidentified… Speechless… Never stood a chance! In remembrance of--… they were always a good--… I'll always love you. Tagged! Step upout of body bags! Keep your mind loaded! No one wants to say, "Rights, rights were what we had". Should've… Would've… Could've… Tagged! Learn your rights to cut daggers on targets waiting on your innocence marked bag. Tagged! Wake up! Reach out of bags! The knowledge you one day would regret you never studied that you had… Tagged! This ain't life or body bags!

The audience clapped and cried. I couldn't stop and chit chat. I had to catch my flight home. The C.S. Café was finally opening tomorrow. It was a Friday night too. I had to check on Brittani as well. I didn't mind if she didn't show because she needed time to grieve. I had called David.

"Hey, I need a favor."

"Wh is it?" He asked.

"Brittani's son was shot and killed. I want to know what I can do to help."

"If there's an ongoing investigation then there's nothing we could do right now."

"Could we set up a rally or march to make sure justice is served."

"Let me call around and get back to you."

Brittani had called me earlier and told me that they were stalling on arresting the officers. There was a camera that caught it all on tape. In that neighborhood everyone had cameras that onlooked their yards. They were trying not to let it get out though. I had to call around for information. I've been through too much hell to sit back and let this nightmare spread like wildfires. I only had myself to give and I had to be there for my friend. I got up and looked through my closet for my outfit to wear for this weekend. I had to have my outfits laid out in advance. Before I knew it, it was already the weekend. I had radio shows and tv shows to attend. I was promoting the opening of the C.S. Café. I had cut the ribbon to the building. The crowd began packing out the building. We were heavily secured. I didn't want anything to happen at the grand opening. I got everyone's attention.

"Good evening everyone. First, I would like to thank you all for coming out and supporting the grand opening of the C.S. Café. Months ago, I never saw this ever being a reality for me. I have lost a lot to be in this moment of success. I stand in front of you, a woman transparent, go ahead and take a look into the overly crowded yet flawed soul of mine. I have nothing to lose."

I looked over to Ty and smiled. I seen the twins hanging out at the bar. Brittani was walking in the club. I was happy to see her yet feeling her pain all at the same time. I needed her and vice versa.

Ch. 45

"This piece is called "Sold".

Sold

      10 pounds, 8 pounds, 5 pounds, sold! Sold into a society I don't even know. $11.50 now centuries later is worth less than a three course meal. Less than the newest weave… Sold! Worthless… Worth less than anything freedom could ever buy. Forced to have relations with Satan's own creation… As sin, the thing they fell so deep in. The hole they drilled to sleep in. Waking up in hard labor… Birth of nations… The crying out of generations… My heritage… Lineage… Sold! My genealogical pathways, Sold! To be in a world that sees me not worth more than the toiletries to stay clean… To be alive in a world that can snatch the same baby you took many of hours to bring into a deceptive world… My baby! My baby! Sold! They tell me they are better off to live somewhere else only to be snatched from freedom by the creation, the spirit Satan grew to rape her day in and day out. I lost a piece of my soul every time they sold my lineage. The numbing feeling seemed to get much easier with every lineage, every baby snatched. Sold! My heritage I came to this place with, I no longer physically carry. Only mere images in my dreams… Waking up sold dreaming to be free… They call this the United States of America but what's so "united", joined together, when every living soul here is no equal? They beat and train to produce better generations like sloppy sequels. Sold! Years later a piece of paper named me free, now my

pride, my spirit, sold! Ideas and inventions I've worked days, weeks, months on sold! A lighter shade was better suited for what I worked hard for as if I wasn't capable, literate enough to invent something useful. Like I didn't have the right to my own project... No wonder my heritage knows not my name... Sold! History untold... The history of this lineage kept getting worse. Sold! Now 1970s, and dreams sold! Compromising roles to be somebody's first... The miseducation... The exploitation of the black folk... Health sold! Sold our own health to crack, cocaine, heroine, and alcohol... Substance given to take away our understanding of surroundings to burn out the gift present within us... To sell our own time with our deepest descendants too dazed to know when being stolen from... Sold! Too many years, memories wasted. Conscience Sold! Too high... Too drunk... Too strung out to free your own self from the substance slave trade you agreed to dose yourself up in... Just decisions sold! Years later are like the years before... Freedom Sold! Imprisoned for imaginary crimes trying to be on the right side of justice... Prison is just a mere form of being judicially owned by "Massa". To stop the rights of some who committed no crime but was suddenly at the wrong place, wrong time or they fit the description of a skin color oblivious to detail and DNA... My rights are sold to the highest paid lawyer and his big expense just to put me away... Sold! Life too far gone to receive anything back... I might get my freedom but memories can't reverse time to let me sit and listen in, watch troubled tears drip from my fresh lineages face like fresh oxygenated blood from fresh gun wounds to the heart. Sold! Killed time... 10,950 days too many... 262,080 hours of should've, could've, would've spent years training up my lineage, heritage, descendants, but I was sold, deep rooted in another slave system to ever get it back. Sold! There are others sold. Many slave systems to get banked off on. Lineages sold... Snatched up on sidewalks... Sold on black markets... Worthless, worth less than a five dollar footlong, that dollar menu from McDonalds, but forced to lie with thieving strays who stay up all night just to taste the crevices of our down unders. Making us mothers way before our time... Pussies only sold to control the mind. Give you a little taste then every time you crawl back they skyrocket the rate. Sold! Worthless, worth less than that ammonia based golden shower he rained down on my face. Sold! Like a caged bird, I'm sold. At times I have the opportunity to be free but my papers of slavery are his fists pounding against me and memories slip too quickly so I stay caged. Sold! Who could really save me anyway? How much? How much for her release? You can buy ten times the sheep but that won't make them leave. Take me! Take me! I'll replace her! They said, "You're too close to the grave to let this one be replaced." Sold! Stuck too far in my own fears to ever let myself go… Sold! Traded to the next highest bidder based off assets genetics made waiting days to escape. Sold! Another part of history left untold because I might not live to build nations foretold. No screaming too bold because once enslaved in my mind, freedom is not there to reach. Justice won't be there to set me free. Sold! Enslaved to the mind! For the rest sold, enslaved to their own sin… To history for some, slavery wasn't a choice and freedom wasn't an option… Today we're sold, keep selling our souls… Too deeply we cut out our own eyes just to lust and feel. Fall deep in their sins, our sins… Sold! So freely we sell our souls denying morality for a sin that feels right. Feels just… God knows I love him! What's love when your vocal chords don't sing it? If you never put fire to actions then how will a person, God ever know you or you him? Sold! How much more can you tie a noose around your neck, be entered by legion (demons of many), and not be freely forgiven? Just take the freedom and start living. Sold! A choice some call a privilege to have. To shackle your own soul is like decades without a bath, use to the feeling, sinus closed to the smell, yet everyone can see your highway to hell. Still to some slavery wasn't a choice and freedom wasn't an option… Your soul's last chance… Run with freedom or Satan's concoction… Too many years, history untold… Choose freedom foretold or slavery, sin, SOLD!

      I finished my piece and I cried. I cried tears of relief. I cried tears of pain. I cried for all of the success that I was standing in and all of the loved ones that I lost to push me here. I had people walk up to me and tell me how they appreciated my work. One girl said that she followed me across the country and she was at my performance for Domestic Mirrors and that made her see herself as it really was. She told me that she freed herself of that situation and is seeking help. It felt good to see people being helped by my own work. I just wished it could have saved me. I wish my work could have saved Sara or my Pops. I left that place and went home. David had pulled me to the side earlier and told me that he had organised a march for justice. Brittani needed this and I was going to be standing by her side until justice was served. I didn't care how long it took. I went home, ate some leftover lasagna, showered, and went to bed. Tomorrow was going to be one of the longest days. Daybreak came and I read my Bible. I had to be prepared for whatever was going to happen. Marches never ended good for people like me. I had seen Jennifer earlier as well talking about Sara. How dare she bring up her name when she wasn't even there for her funeral. As I was putting on my clothes, I looked over at that letter. It was thick as a hoagie. I didn't open it. I was more scared of what it would say. I didn't know what she had wrote. I just wanted it to be a secret written on paper, It was eating away at me to not know what she had written. I didn't open it. I got up and got ready for the march. We marched down 16th St downtown. His dad's family held a march on California. We had signs that read "My life matters too you know." We marched all down that street. We marched down 20th St S. We marched down University Blvd. We needed to be heard. We couldn't keep having our babies killed because of an invisible fear. Their fears were like Casper the friendly ghost. They weren't real. Now people of all races have those people who will kill for anything. Those people you fear. A twelve year old who was just trying to answer his dad's phone call did not deserve to be murdered. We all cried while joining hands. I looked at Brittani. I had to hold her a little tighter so she wouldn't pass out. We ended our march at the 16th St Baptist Church. We passed out petitions to get that officer and others fired. Every evidence backed it up. I guess no one was listening. They heard clearly; they just acted like they were deaf.

"Are you okay Britt?" I asked.

"I will be, right? It feels like someone just cut my heart out. They put it back in but it only beats at fourty percent." She replied.

"I know the pain hurts. We might not have the same pain. It hurts nonetheless. I wish I could carry your pain."

"You've carried too much as it is. I don't see how you aren't falling apart right now."

"It's called a mother who won't give up. You can't give up. You have another son who needs you now more than ever. You have to push through. Promise me that you won't make him suffer." I said.

"I can't promise you anything but I'll try."

We hugged each other and parted ways. I had to go home and pack for California. I was going to Spoken Funk to perform "Slave Mentality. I had a lot ahead of me to do but I needed to not cry right now.

Ch. 46

The twins had picked me up this time. We all were heading to Shuttlesworth Airport to LAX. I had to keep gum on me to keep my ears from popping. It always felt like I had an ongoing ear infection when that happened. I fell asleep on the plane. We had first class so I always chose the window seat so I had something to lean my head on. The flight attendant woke me up when we had landed. While David and I got our luggage, Daniel rented the SUV. We stayed at Aunt Bert's house. Bert was short for Alberta and and she will be quick to curse you out. Alberta was your old school grandma. I loved her though. We only stayed there long enough to drop off our luggage. We got back into the vehicle and drove to the venue. It was packed. It had way more people than I could imagine. The host was a tall slender man. He had a limp from fighting in Iraq. He introduced me.

"Wow it's good to be in Cali. I can't believe this is the last stop of my tour. I have certainly grown over the last couple of months. Summer is now."

Some point I was happy that the tour was over so that some part of my life could slow down. In another way, my escape was coming to an end. I had the film so we'd have to see.

"This piece is called "Slave Mentality". I hope you like it."

Slave Mentality

Slave ... You runaway trying to find the meaning of "north" in your life... Getting out of the ghetto just to downgrade the same types of people you left behind... Like your profit isn't geared to making us your stringed puppet... As of you're out ventriloquist... Like we speak the same... Think the same... Put money into the same thing that eighty percent of your race is shackled in... Conditioning our future that hoes and money is what is expected to live and die for... You're just their Uncle Tom... The run tell massa... The snitch that will still get shot of a lie caught the back of your head from one of them like Rosewood's history taught you nothing boy... Like your fantasy of lies never taught you that they spread like burning wildfires in a quiet forest... Instead of rebuilding our education, you'd rather franchise off of materialistic waste... Like gold from the hidden parts of the earth boobie trapped to make you sure you did before you leave with it... Got these boys killing because their daddy made his own mistake and walked out... Slave... They posted you up like a headless mannequin in a department store on display for the materialistic shit you're wearing... Decapitated like Maria Antoinette... Got you thinking you're immortal 'cause you just got a statue but don't even know your statute of limitations...Slave... They got you so blind that they can revoke your freedom for using the same illegal substance they stay addicted to at their own house parties... Like money make convictions fall on deaf ears...Slave... Got you playing the fence on different shades of your ancestors like they aren't laughing already because they made it that way... You mean to tell me you won't date a dark skinned girl or a fat one like your mamma wasn't the posted symbol for Aunt Jemima but you love her nonetheless... They got you hating the way your face shaped... Second guessing an original vintage work of art... Slave... You can't even see you're just the messsenger delivering me the false hope of peace but you think since you're the messenger you're now the "Almighty"... Slave ... As if it wasn't already worse to hear deaf ears, fall on convictio's but you turn to black on black crime... They've already been convicted!... You turn to outfits and backgrounds like our babies needed a background check to live in America... Not live as in stay but leave as in breathe... Slave... You can't see that you still ain't free... You're too clenched to your mi,d to announce the injustice... If it ain't hoes and sex, I guess I should keep your name out of it... I just did because slavee is you rebranded... Your mentality has been altered... Damaged... Deterred... Take a detour the hard way... Making money for the same ones that can have you killed... Make it look like it was suicide... Slave... Headless... Taught not to wake up with your head so they tell you whatever isn't for everybody... Drink the kool-aid... It's true... While you're looking for your last freedom, your slave mentality just killed you

I finished my set and I bowed. The audience clapped and cheered. We headed back to the house to get some rest before we headed back home. Daybreak came and we were on the road headed to LAX then to Shutttlesworth. We made it back late that night. I went in my house and I dropped my bags and turned on the alarm. I ran upstairs to my room, shut the door, fell to the floor and cried. I stood up and grabbed the letter Sara left me. I promised myself that whatever was written in this letter that I would just let go. The letter read, "Dear Christina, if you are reading this then something horrible has happened. I know you would be the strong one of us all. Thomas and I was going down the wrong road so fast. I guess I didn't leave because I didn't want to be a statistic and end up divorced. I knew you would choose the children if push came to shove. I hope they are fine. I bet they are getting big. Kiss them for me. At this point I had to find strength of my own. I killed Thomas before writing this letter. I had to get you out of the room before I bashed his head in with my gun. I finally shot that bastard! I had to find the courage from somewhere. I didn't want to go to jail for this. Before I pulled this trigger, I wanted you to know that I love you. I know you would make a better mother. Ty's a good man. He'll come around. Goodbye my friend. Sisters for life."

"Sisters for life!" I whispered.

I cried. I didn't know if this is what I wanted to hear. I didn't know how to accept this. How do you accept your best friend telling you she committed suicide? I stood up and walked over to the bed and laid beside Tyler. I cried on his chest. He looked down, pushed my chin up and kissed me. To be honest, I don't know what life has for me. I don't know how far success was going to take me or how much I'd have to sacrifice to get to it. All I know is that I have a great support system. Pain never defined me, it just elevated me to a sweeter success story.

Printed in the United States
By Bookmasters